"Okay, so you're not from the agency, Ms. Delaney. But can you stay for just a while and help me straighten out my adopted sister? She may not know it, but she needs a woman around."

Suddenly Megan remembered the purpose of this trip. Meg knew she was crazy to do this, but somehow the words just came out. "If you want me to stay, I'll try it for a few weeks."

"Darlin', I want you to stay so bad, you can name your own price." His deep voice rippled sexily and warmth rushed through her.

"Oh, no. I can't accept money." For heaven's sake—if only he knew! "I could use a place—"

"It's a deal, but I'm going to do my best to talk you into staying longer...."

Dear Reader,

This month, Silhouette Romance is celebrating the classic love story. That intensely romantic, emotional and compelling novel you just can't resist. And leading our month of classic love stories is *Wife without a Past* by Elizabeth Harbison, a deeply felt tale of an amnesiac wife who doesn't recognize the FABULOUS FATHER she'd married....

Pregnant with His Child... by bestselling author Carla Cassidy will warm your heart as a man is reunited with the child he never knew existed—and the woman he never stopped loving. Next, our MEN! promotion continues, as Silhouette Romance proves a good man isn't hard to find in *The Stranger's Surprise* by Laura Anthony. In Patricia Thayer's moving love story, *The Cowboy's Convenient Bride,* a woman turns up at a Texas ranch with a very poignant secret. And in *Plain Jane Gets Her Man* by Robin Wells, you'll be delighted by the modern-day Cinderella who wins the man of her dreams. Finally, Lisa Kaye Laurel's wonderful miniseries, ROYAL WEDDINGS, continues with *The Prince's Baby.*

As the Thanksgiving holiday approaches, I'd like to give a special thanks to all of you, the readers, for making Silhouette Romance such a popular and beloved series of books. Enjoy November's titles!

Regards,

Melissa Senate
Senior Editor
Silhouette Books

Please address questions and book requests to:
Silhouette Reader Service
U.S.: 3010 Walden Ave., P.O. Box 1325, Buffalo, NY 14269
Canadian: P.O. Box 609, Fort Erie, Ont. L2A 5X3

THE COWBOY'S CONVENIENT BRIDE

Patricia Thayer

Silhouette

ROMANCE™

Published by Silhouette Books

America's Publisher of Contemporary Romance

FOR THE BIRTHDAY LUNCH GROUP. MY
SISTERS-IN-LAW, SHEILA, SUSIE, BETH, MARY
AND PAT. THANKS FOR YOUR FRIENDSHIP
AND SUPPORT AND FOR NEVER COUNTING
THE CANDLES.

 SILHOUETTE BOOKS

ISBN 0-373-19261-4

THE COWBOY'S CONVENIENT BRIDE

Copyright © 1997 by Patricia Wright

This edition published by arrangement with Harlequin Books S.A.

Printed in U.S.A.

Books by Patricia Thayer

Silhouette Romance

Just Maggie #895
Race to the Altar #1009
The Cowboy's Courtship #1064
Wildcat Wedding #1086
Reilly's Bride #1146
The Cowboy's Convenient Bride #1261

Silhouette Special Edition

Nothing Short of a Miracle #1116

PATRICIA THAYER

Patricia has been writing for eleven years and has published seven books with Silhouette. Her books have been nominated for the National Readers' Choice Award, Virginia Romance Writers of America's Holt Medallion and the prestigious RITA Award. Pat has been a longtime member of the Orange County chapter of RWA, served on the board and was elected copresident in 1995.

Thanks to the understanding men in her life—her husband, Steve, and three sons—Pat has been able to fulfill her dream of writing romance. She loves to hear from readers. You can write her at P.O. Box 6251, Anaheim, CA 92816-0251.

Chapter One

The Stone Ranch was as big as Megan Delaney remembered.

She climbed out of her car and looked off toward the pristine white outer buildings. Two were horse barns, the other a covered arena that produced some of the best stock in the area, her daddy had once told her. Meg sighed. Was she making a mistake coming back to Mineral Wells? It had been thirteen years since her family left Texas.

Meg drew a long breath and released it as more childhood memories came flooding back. None of which were good. Her daddy had made sure of that. She focused again on the Stoner house, wondering, as she had once during her two-hour drive from Boswell, Oklahoma, just what she would say once she got back here.... Maybe she should have just made a phone call to find out what she needed to know.

No! Three weeks ago, she'd promised her mother she would come in person. And everyone knew that Meg never broke her promises, especially not this one. It had been her mother's last request, her last words.

Meg fought back tears, recalling her mother's passing only three weeks ago. Nina Delaney's death hadn't been a surprise to the family, but that didn't lessen the sadness. The forty-five-year-old woman had been suffering from cancer, and toward the end it had been a blessing when she finally found peace.

Meg glanced toward the house, knowing there was just one more thing to take care of before closing the door on her past. She reached for her purse and started up the walkway.

After today she would concentrate on her future. She would finally have the chance to get on with her own life. For the past twenty-four years she had been giving to everyone else. It was time for her.

But first she had to find out if her younger sister was healthy and happy. A younger sister Meg had thought dead. She'd been shocked when her mother confessed the thirteen-year-old secret on her deathbed. All these years no one ever told Meg the truth about the baby girl that had been given up for adoption. Given up or sold to the wealthy Stoner family. Sold to the highest bidder. And what did they get in return? A farm that barely yielded an existence.

Climbing up the steps to the porch, Meg quickly smoothed the wrinkles from her tan slacks and red short-sleeve sweater. With a shaky hand, she lifted the brass knocker three times, then paced nervously, practicing what she was going to say to Mr. and Mrs. Stoner. Legally she couldn't demand to see her sister. *Sister.* The word sounded strange. So many years she longed for a sister, someone to take her side against her two brothers, Clint and Rick. Once again she cursed her daddy for what he'd done.

Suddenly the door jerked open and Meg bit back a gasp, surprised by the large man standing in the doorway. His coal black hair hung defiantly over his forehead as hooded dark eyes stared at her. His clean-shaven square jaw already showed a hint of a shadow. Dressed in a white shirt that accented broad shoulders and a flat stomach, his hands were braced on his slim hips. The tight-fitting jeans he wore were adorned by a black belt and silver buckle. Linc Stoner was even more handsome than she remembered.

"It's about time you got here," he said, suddenly reaching for her hand and pulling her inside the house. "I needed you an hour ago."

"Excuse me," Meg choked, shivering in the sudden coolness of the dark entry, or it might have been the effect this man standing so close had on her. "I think you've made a mistake."

He raised his hand. "Please, don't say that. You're my last hope. I've already had two quit on me. I need you."

Meg's mouth gaped open as he gave her a pleading look. His eyes were so dark, so compelling. When she realized she was staring, she rushed to explain. "Wait! You don't understand—"

"Look, I promise, if you agree to stay, I'll make it worth your while. I'll pay double. Come on. The old biddy from Social Services is waiting."

Meg's head was spinning. She was having trouble making sense of the situation. How could she, with Linc Stoner's arm across her shoulders, the scent of his musk cologne teasing her? All she could do was allow him to guide her into the living room. On the sofa sat a woman probably in her fifties dressed in a dark suit, her gray hair pulled back into a tight bun.

"See, I told you she would be here," Linc offered. "Mrs. Simpson, I'd like you to meet Miss..." He frowned at Meg.

"Meg Delaney," Meg quickly finished as she watched the stoic woman stand.

"Mr. Stoner—" Mrs. Simpson nodded, then glanced at the file in her hands "—as I told you earlier, a tutor isn't enough. Nicole is going to need adult supervision twenty-four hours a day."

Nicole. Was that her sister's name? Meg wondered as she glanced around the room. Where were the Stoners?

The caseworker turned to Linc. "Since your parents are deceased, and you haven't been able to handle your sister's…needs, the court has no alternative but to put her in a home."

"No!" Linc said firmly. Looking frustrated, he lowered his voice. "Excuse me, Mrs. Simpson. Didn't I tell you that Ms. Delaney has also agreed to live in, to help supervise my sister's activities?"

The older woman didn't hide her displeasure as she turned toward Meg. "Is this true, Ms. Delaney?"

Meg's gaze darted back and forth between Mrs. Simpson and Linc, her head buzzing with questions. What was going to happen to her sister? Her instincts told her one thing—staying might not be a bad idea. "Yes, I could stay for a while, but—"

"Well, Ms. Delaney," the caseworker interrupted. "I'll need to know about your work experience."

"Experience?"

"Yes, you need to be able to tutor Nicole."

Meg swallowed as she glanced back and forth between Linc and Mrs. Simpson. "Well, I was a teacher's aid in Boswell, Oklahoma. And I did help tutor my brothers through high school." That was true.

The woman just looked at her, then quickly wrote down some notes. "You seem awfully young."

Linc stepped in. "I didn't realize that being over thirty was required for a tutor."

The older woman didn't even look up. "Well, Ms. Delaney, I don't envy you your job. Just make sure that I get a written report weekly on Nicole's progress. I'll also be contacting the school district on your qualifications." The woman gathered up her things and prepared to leave. "I'll be in touch."

The sound of the door closing created an intimate silence between the only two people left in the room. Meg looked at Linc and a warm tingle rushed though her, making her feel much like the eleven-year-old girl who had once been infatuated with him, when he was a handsome sixteen-year-old boy. He didn't remember her, but why should he? she thought with a twinge of disappointment.

He smiled, showing off even white teeth. "I can't tell you how grateful I am. You saved my hide. I swear that woman is after blood."

"It sounds like she's just doing her job," Meg returned, wondering when the time would be right to tell him the real reason she had come here.

Linc sobered quickly. "Taking Nikki out of the only home she's ever known isn't what I call doing her job."

"Would you mind telling me why Mrs. Simpson is trying to remove your...sister?"

He grimaced and walked across the room to the front of the long camel-colored leather sofa facing the stone fireplace. "Like Mrs. Simpson said, our parents were killed six months ago in a car accident and Nikki hasn't been dealing with it very well. She's gotten into a few scrapes lately."

"What kind of scrapes?"

Linc shrugged his wide shoulders. "She's been ditching school a lot, and when she does go she's been disruptive." He turned away and raked his hand through his hair. "Now the principal won't let her return until she has some counseling. So while I'm waiting for some shrink to tell her she misses her mom and daddy, Nikki is falling behind with her schoolwork. She needs a tutor to keep up."

She knew he was leaving out a lot. Social Services didn't get involved just because a student was behind in algebra.

Meg heard a slight noise and sensed the presence of someone behind her. Slowly she turned to find a dark-haired girl standing in the wide archway.

This was her sister, Meg thought excitedly.

A sister she didn't know existed just three short weeks ago. She was unable to breathe as her gaze eagerly combed over the tall, coltish thirteen-year-old.

Nikki Stoner was dressed in a red skirt that hit her mid-thigh and a T-shirt that was cut off just below her budding bustline. Blinking rapidly to fight the tears, Meg searched her face, and although her coloring was darker, there was no doubt about the family resemblance. Nikki looked like their mother and grandmother. Meg's heart raced. She had a sister. But her enthusiasm swiftly died because she couldn't say anything. At least not yet.

Nikki's sullen gaze connected with Meg's, then the teenager gave her a cool once-over. "Another teacher?"

"Her name is Ms. Delaney, Nikki. And, yes, she has agreed to tutor you."

"I don't want her here."

"That's too bad," Linc said. "Ms. Delaney has also agreed to stay with us. So you better get used to it."

Nikki glared at her brother. "I hate you!" she screamed. "I hate you!" Then she turned and ran from the room.

Meg had to fight the urge to go after her. Instead she looked at an embarrassed Linc.

"Not the loving family you expected, huh?"

"It's obvious there's a problem when a social worker has to intervene."

Linc Stoner stared at the attractive blonde across the room. Was he making a mistake hiring someone so young? Meg Delaney couldn't be more than twenty-two, twenty-three. He could have sworn she sounded older on the phone. Well, it wasn't like he had a lot of applications to choose from. "A few months ago we were a close family.

But since our parents' death last October, Nikki has been like this. I know she's hurting but…''

His gaze locked with Meg's and he caught the compassion in her wide brown eyes. He nearly lost his train of thought. ''She's been angry with everyone. She's alienated her friends…me. I've grounded her, but she only rebels more. Then she got in trouble in town by shoplifting. Luckily I knew the store owner and he didn't press charges—the first time. The second time it happened, I was out of town on business and she was taken to the police station when they couldn't get a hold of me.''

Linc clenched his fists as he began to pace. He'd never felt so helpless in his life. ''I'm at the end of my rope,'' he said. ''The principal won't allow her back in school until I can guarantee she'll behave. I hired tutors, but Nikki refused to cooperate and the women quit. Then two weeks ago Nikki ran away. I was terrified and had no choice but to call the sheriff to help find her. That's when Social Services got involved.'' He skirted the large pine coffee table as he came to stand in front of Meg. ''You may be my last chance.''

Meg's lungs momentarily refused to work. As soon as she was able to speak, she had to tell him the truth. But, darn, he was a hard man to resist. She found herself actually thinking about staying. After all, Nikki was her sister. ''I don't know…''

''I'll triple your pay.'' The amount he mentioned made her gasp. ''And you get free room and board,'' he added. ''At least will you give it a try?''

Meg's head was spinning. Her friend Cathy in Fort Worth was expecting her. And she had a job interview next week. A life. But the promise she'd made to her mother echoed in her head as she glanced toward the stairs. Suddenly there was a lump in her throat. How could she leave when her sister needed her?

''Look, Mr. Stoner…''

"It's Linc." He smiled at her and her heart sank into her stomach, making it more difficult for her to explain.

"Linc, I'm not who you think I am. I'm not from the agency."

The telephone rang before he had the chance to say anything. He excused himself and answered the call. The quiet conversation didn't help calm Meg's nerves. If she told him the truth, Linc Stoner would throw her out the door.

He hung up the phone, turned around, folding his arms across his chest. "That was the agency. The tutor they sent out had car trouble. They want to reschedule." One dark eyebrow rose and Meg found she had the urge to soothe the wrinkles in his forehead.

"Who are you, Meg Delaney? Why are you here?"

Meg swallowed, "My mother...she's just recently died..."

"I'm sorry."

She caught a trace of pain in his eyes. "Thank you." She quickly looked away from his mesmerizing gaze and took a needed breath. "I was on my way to Fort Worth, and I...I just stopped by to see your parents. I'm sorry. I didn't know about the accident."

He nodded. "Oh, so your mother and Pauline were friends?"

"They knew each other a long time ago," Meg said, assuming the two women had met at least once.

"Well, Pauline had a lot of friends," he said proudly. "She was active in the community and church. Dad used to say it was because we spent so much time with the stock and shows."

"Your parents sound like nice people."

"The best," he agreed, but quickly got back to business. "Well, Ms. Delaney, it looks like the placement agency has let me down. But you may be a gift from heaven. You're certainly qualified. Can you stay and help me

straighten out my sister? Believe me, Nikki may not know
it, but she really needs a woman around.''

Meg knew she was crazy to do this, but somehow the
words just came out. ''I'm not sure if I can help much,
but if you still want me to, I'll give it a try for a few
weeks.''

''Darlin', I need you to stay so bad, you can name your
own price.'' His deep voice rippled sexily, and warmth
rushed through her.

''Oh, no. I can't accept money.'' For heaven's sake,
Nikki was her sister. And the girl needed her. ''But I could
use a place to stay until—''

He didn't let her finish. ''It's a deal, but I'm going to
do my best to talk you into staying longer.'' He pointed a
finger in her direction. ''Then we'll seriously talk about
your pay, Ms. Delaney.''

''Please, call me Meg,'' she said.

''It's sure good to meet you, Meg.'' He reached for her
hand and cupped it in his rough one. ''I'll have one of the
ranch hands bring in your luggage.'' He checked his
watch. ''I'm sorry, I have to leave. I need to get a mare
to the Reynolds' ranch.'' He released her hand and started
out of the room. ''I'll be back by supper.''

''But...'' Meg glanced toward the stairs. ''Which room
do I use?''

Linc reached for a straw Stetson hanging on a hook by
the door. ''Choose any one you want.''

''B-but...'' She was stuttering. ''What if it belongs to
someone else?'' Which bedroom was his, she wondered,
and shivered at the thought.

''There's not much chance of that with six bedrooms in
this house. Take the one at the head of the stairs.'' He
looked her over and she felt her knees weaken. ''It seems
to suit you.''

''Are you sure I'm not putting anyone out?''

Linc gave her a strange look as he placed his hat on his

head and tugged it forward. "Darlin', I'd move into the barn and give you my room if you can help Nikki."

"I don't think that will be necessary."

"Wait until you get to know Nikki better. She might change your mind." He tossed her a grin and headed out the door.

In her new bedroom, Meg ran her fingers over the pink floral comforter trimmed with an eyelet border. There was a mountain of pillows against the white wrought iron headboard, and on either side of the bed, matching tables were accented with blue pottery lamps. She turned around and caught her reflection in the mirror over the cherry dresser.

What was she doing here? She didn't belong in a fancy house, with fancy furniture. Meg glanced down at the thick carpet under her feet and thought about the cold bare floor in the small house back home, the tiny bedroom she had shared with her brothers until she got older and needed privacy. She never did have any, sleeping on the worn sofa. The only good thing was that she had the warmest spot in the house with the wood-burning stove only a few feet away. Of course, she'd also been the one who had to get up and keep it stoked.

Meg walked to the windows overlooking the backyard. She pulled the sheer curtains aside and glanced down at the large patio area. It wasn't the beautiful rose garden or the perfectly manicured lawn that held her attention. It was the swimming pool. The cooling-off, soothe-your-aching-muscles, playtime, crystal-clear-water pool. Not the stream back of the barn, which most of the time seemed to be more mud than water.

Meg dropped the curtain and sat down on the window seat. Nikki had had such a different life than she and her brothers. She froze. Clint and Rick. What would they think if they knew about Nikki? Since her mother had made her promise not to tell anyone before she checked on Nikki, her brothers had no idea she was stopping off at the Stoner Ranch. All they knew was that she was headed to Fort Worth for a job interview. Now she had to call and let them know about her change of plans. Meg glanced around her new bedroom. Boy, Clint and Rick would never believe this.

Meg's thoughts went to her father. She hadn't had much respect for Ralph Delaney, with his drinking and shiftlessness. Although she'd been only an adolescent when he died, she was the oldest, which meant she had to help her mother keep the family together. Meg hadn't hated being poor as much as she hated the loss of dignity, having to go on welfare after her father's death.

For years Meg had worked hard, finally making the farm profitable. It had always been a struggle, but with the help of part-time jobs, she managed to keep the farm going and her brothers in school. That was the one thing she had been proud of.

Nikki had grown up differently. The girl had never known poverty, but she had known, all too well, what it was like to lose loved ones. Meg knew she could help these people. Her decision to stay started to make even more sense. There was a knock on the door and Meg stood. "Come in."

An elderly, heavyset woman with white hair peered in.

"Hello, I'm Dora, the housekeeper, cook, and, well, just about anything that needs to be done around here falls in my lap." She smiled. "Linc told me you were gonna be staying a while. Is there anything you need?"

Meg smiled. "Oh, no. I just wonder if you might need my help with supper."

Dora's gray eyes sparkled. "Not really, but if you'd like to come down and keep me company, I wouldn't mind at all." The woman glanced across the hall. "Doesn't look like her majesty is gonna come out of her room anytime soon. Just as well. Nikki's moods aren't suitable for company." The housekeeper turned and walked away.

That evening Meg sat at the dining room table across from a sullen Nicole, who was busy forming a river basin out of her mashed potatoes. At the far end of the trestle table sat Linc. He'd showered and changed into a fresh shirt and jeans, but his immediate interest appeared to be Dora's pot roast. Meg was still too nervous to have much of an appetite. Her mind kept turning to her deception and the young girl across from her. She had to focus on getting to know her sister.

"Nicole, maybe after dinner you and I can get together and discuss your lesson plan," Meg said, hoping the girl would start talking to her.

The teenager looked up from her plate and glared at Meg. "You're so smart, you figure it out."

"Nikki," Linc warned. "Ms. Delaney is only trying to help."

"Please, call me Meg."

Nicole jumped to her feet. "I'm not going to call you anything, because I don't want you here. So just leave."

Meg stood, too. "I'm not going anywhere, Nicole," she began, trying to keep her voice calm. "I'm here to help you with your studies, so get used to it."

Nicole looked close to tears and Meg wanted to go around the table and hug her.

Suddenly Nicole turned to her brother. "Why are you doing this to me? Haven't you done enough?" She threw her napkin on the table and ran from the room.

"Nicole Stoner, you get back here," Linc bellowed as he got up from the table and started after her.

Meg stopped him. "Please, let her go. She's had a lot to deal with."

"Don't you think I know that?" Linc rubbed the bridge of his nose in frustration. When he turned toward Meg, she could see the strain on his face. "She hates me," he said in a choked voice.

Meg ached to reach out and comfort him. Instead she tried a few words. "She just hates everybody because she's hurting."

"But I can't reach her. We used to be so close. There isn't anything I wouldn't do for her. We were more than just brother and sister. We were best buddies, too."

"You still are. She feels close enough to vent her anger at you. It happened to my brothers when our daddy died."

He looked at her, with a faint light of hope showing in his brown eyes. "What did you do?"

She felt the warm tingle of his gaze all the way down her spine. She glanced away. "I just hung in there. But I let them know I didn't appreciate their bad behavior. They spent a lot of time doing extra chores."

"Outside of taking care of her horse, Nikki hasn't had to do much besides her schoolwork."

"Maybe you shouldn't let her ride until her behavior changes."

Linc once again looked frustrated. "That's another problem. Nikki hasn't even stepped into the barn since the accident. Before, we worked nearly every day to get her ready for the junior quarter horse shows. Her horse, Sweet Sue, should have placed high this spring." He puffed out a long breath. "Now Pedro is working the animal, but Sweetie doesn't react the same without Nikki."

Nicole has her own horse, Meg thought, just a little envious. All her life she had dreamed of owning a horse. The closest she'd come was when she used to help her daddy when he was training cutters. She'd gotten to cool them down, groom them, muck out stalls, and as a reward, she occasionally got to ride. Of course, Ralph Delaney had only worked when he sobered up enough to keep a job. Her father had always talked about breeding his own stock.

Her father had possessed a special touch with the animals. If only he could have stopped the drinking.

Meg was brought back to the present when Dora appeared before her. "Would you like some coffee?"

"Yes, thank you," Meg answered gratefully.

Linc followed Dora and took two cups from the housekeeper. "Come on, it's cooler on the patio," he said. He didn't wait for Meg's answer but led her through the French doors off the living room.

Linc set the coffee cups on the glass-top table and pulled out a chair for Meg. He watched her take a seat, realizing that since she had arrived today she seemed to tense up every time he got near her.

He smiled to himself as he took a sip of coffee and studied the pretty woman seated across the table. Maybe it was for the best if Meg Delaney kept her distance. He didn't need to get involved with Nikki's tutor. She was an employee. An employee he needed to keep for his sister's sake. He couldn't complicate things. Nikki's problems were his main concern.

But that didn't keep him from wondering if Meg Delaney's long honey blond hair was as soft as it looked. Did her chestnut eyes change color when she was aroused? His gaze lowered to her blouse, which highlighted her high, round breasts. The rest was hidden by the table and her long skirt. He'd only had a glimpse of her trim ankles, but it had been enough for him to imagine they were attached to a pair of long, shapely legs.

He felt his body reacting but assured himself that it was only because it had been months since he'd been with a woman—not since he and Susanne had decided to go their separate ways. Susanne liked a good time and hadn't wanted the responsibility of a teenager. But Nikki was his sister, for Christ's sake. Maybe not by blood, but he couldn't love her any less.

Damn! If he could only turn back the clock. Linc stared

at the pool as a warm breeze rippled the water, carrying the soft scent of jasmine through the air. If only he hadn't been away with Susanne that weekend. He never should have let her talk him into going away for the weekend instead of flying his parents down to San Antonio. He should have been at the horse auction anyway. He and his dad were partners. Not being there for them was something he would regret forever.

"Are you all right?"

He shook his head. "What?"

"I asked if you're all right," Meg repeated. "If you're having second thoughts about asking me to stay…"

"No! That's not it." He saw the concern in her eyes. "It's just been a long day. Hell, it's been a long week." He relaxed back in the chair. His eyes met hers and he suddenly realized how lonely he'd been lately. "I guess I'm missing my parents. We used to sit here by the pool all the time. Dad had it put in when Nikki was five. She said she wanted to swim, and the next week the contractors were out here giving bids."

"Sounds like they loved her a lot."

"From the moment she came home from the hospital," he agreed. "I guess it was that they'd waited so long for a child, and when Nikki came along…" Linc remembered the day the baby girl arrived. He, too, fell in love with his sister the moment he laid eyes on her. Nikki completed the family he'd never had before the Stoners took him in. Now, if he didn't do something, he might lose it all.

He stood. "Look, I'm sorry, but I better call it a night." He knew he was too restless to sleep, but he couldn't sit still either. "I need to get up early. But don't let me keep you from sitting out here as long as you like."

Meg's eyes locked with his and he almost changed his mind. But he couldn't. Linc started across the brick patio, then stopped. "Meg, just don't let Nikki get away with anything. I love my sister but she is a master at manipulating people. She needs someone to be firm with her."

Meg got up from her chair. "I think my brothers would attest to the fact that I can be firm."

He nodded, wanting to believe her. "I'm paying you a lot of money."

She straightened her back, and there was no doubting the anger in her eyes. "I thought I made it clear that I would only accept room and board. If you're having second thoughts, Mr. Stoner, I can leave." When he didn't say anything immediately, she started toward the door.

Linc reached out and grabbed her by the arm. When she turned and faced him he saw the hurt and stubbornness on her face, and, oddly, it reminded him of Nikki. "I'm sorry, Meg. I'm just worried that my sister won't make it through this. If the courts take her..."

Meg placed her hand on his arm, and heat surged through his skin like an electrical charge. "We won't let them. We'll get Nikki through this."

God, how he wanted to believe in her, in her optimism. "You don't understand," he started, then turned away. "Nikki and I aren't blood relatives. We were both adopted by the Stoners." He saw her surprised look. "I was already a teenager and my dad couldn't have cared less what happened to me when the Stoners took me in. But Nikki was adopted as an infant."

Meg's eyes widened in surprise. "That shouldn't make any difference."

"It might if Nikki's biological family ever found out about her problems. They might show up on my doorstep and want her back."

Chapter Two

Meg hadn't slept much, thinking about what Linc had said to her last night. Should she take a chance and tell him the truth? He would either let her stay and help or toss her out the door and out of Nicole's life.

When she finally climbed out of bed it was nearly six o'clock. In the shower, with the hot water running down her back, she had come to a decision. More than anything she wanted to get to know her baby sister. So she wouldn't tell Linc the truth. Not yet.

After making her bed, she hurried downstairs and through the imposing dining room into the cheerful kitchen. She stopped to admire the glossy white cupboards and rose-colored tile. There was a large oak table and six ladder-back chairs in front of a bay window overlooking the side yard and the horse corral.

Dora appeared from the pantry. "Well, good mornin'. What can I fix you for breakfast?"

"I'll just wait on everyone else."

The housekeeper grinned. "Linc had breakfast two hours ago and has been in the arena ever since. Doubt we'll see him until lunch. And there's no telling when Nikki will get up."

"Does she always stay in her room so much?"

"Since the accident. Before that she was always down here pestering everyone." The housekeeper smiled. "She loved being with her mama. They used to like to bake." The woman brought Meg a cup of coffee and motioned for her to sit down.

Meg sank into a chair by the table. "Linc told me Nikki spent a lot of time with her horse."

"Yeah, that child's daddy sat her on a horse before she could walk. I still remember the little spotted pony she had. Then a few years ago at Christmas they gave her Sweetie. A beautiful chestnut mare with mighty impressive bloodlines. There was nothin' too good for little Nicole Stoner. Her daddy and brother made sure of that."

"It sounds like you don't approve of the way she was raised."

Dora shook her head. "I've been around this family for nearly thirty years, and I've never been known for holding my tongue. Nikki's spoiled. I know the child has had a rough time of it lately, but her mama would be ashamed if she were here to see her behavior." The housekeeper wiped her hands on her apron. "What Nikki needs is—"

"I'm Nikki's tutor," Meg interrupted, not wanting to hear any more derogatory things about her sister. "I'm not a psychologist. But I do hope I can help her get through this by being her friend." She stood. "I better go and get her so we can start to work."

"Fine, but I doubt she's awake."

Meg ignored Dora's warning as she walked out and went up the stairs. Going to the bedroom she'd been told was Nikki's, she knocked softly. No answer. She knocked again, harder. Then again.

"Nikki, it's Meg. Time to wake up. We need to get started on your schoolwork."

She heard muffled sounds coming from beyond the door. Then, a little more clearly, "Go away."

Meg sighed. "Come on, Nikki, wake up."

"Go away."

Meg tried the doorknob and discovered it locked. "Open the door, Nikki."

This time there was complete silence. "All right, you want to play games, I'll play." Meg turned on her heels and went downstairs and into the kitchen. The housekeeper looked up from the sink and, seeing Meg alone, smiled knowingly.

"I told you."

She wasn't in the mood for I told you so. "Dora, you said Linc was working in the arena?"

"That's where he said he'd be."

Meg walked out the door, picking up her stride as she marched determinedly toward the huge covered arena. Once inside, the cool air was almost a shock, but it felt good. The familiar odor of straw and horses assaulted her, making her feel right at home. A quick glance around at all the activity told her there weren't any idle hands on the Stoner Ranch. Several quarter horses in the arena were being worked through various stages of training. She moved toward the corral railing and stood on the bottom rung, looking over the large dirt arena. A beautiful roan mare caught her eye, and she was soon mesmerized by the sight of the magnificent animal being taken through her reining drill.

"May I help you, ma'am?"

Meg looked over her shoulder and found herself looking into the blue eyes of a man around her age. He pulled off his hat, revealing thick blond hair.

Meg climbed down from the railing. "Sorry, I got distracted. She's a beautiful horse."

He nodded toward the animal in question. "Flame. We

hope she'll distract a few judges too.'' His glance swung
back to Meg, and he waited for her to speak.

"I need to see Linc.''

Tiny lines appeared around his eyes as he smiled.
"Well, he's pretty busy right now. Maybe I can help you.''

Meg wondered if his knowing grin meant there were a
lot of women who just dropped by to see Linc. "I'm Meg
Delaney, Nikki's tutor, and I really need to talk to him.''

The smile disappeared. "Sure, Ms. Delaney. I'm Dale
Harris, the foreman here. Linc is at the far end of the arena.
He'll be working Devil in a second.''

"I don't want to bother him. I just need to ask him a
quick question, that's all.'' Meg climbed back up on the
railing and peered toward the far end, where she spied Linc
coming into the arena astride a coal black stallion.

He was dressed in a tan fitted Western shirt and jeans.
His hat was pulled low on his head and he held the reins
loosely in his gloved hands, poised and in control as the
horse closed up the figure eight, then eased into a walk as
they moved toward the end of the arena. Meg glanced
around and saw that some of the hands had stopped their
chores to watch the magnificent man and beast put on a
show. And what a show it was.

Meg watched as both rider and horse worked expertly
together. Smoothly, efficiently, the horse gained momentum with each stride as they raced across the arena. In-
stantly, on a predetermined spot, Linc gave his horse slack,
then said "whoa" in a firm voice, pulling back lightly on
the reins.

As if he were built with a hinge in his powerful loins,
the horse folded his hindquarters under him, melting into
the ground, his momentum carrying him into a spectacular
slide. Meg glanced down at the perfectly aligned tracks,
the "11" that was so coveted by reiners.

"Perfect." Meg sighed.

Suddenly Linc looked in her direction. Meg felt a jolt,

now doubting that she should have come to bother Linc and instead should have handled the situation with Nikki on her own. Too late. He tugged on the reins and turned the horse in her direction.

"What's wrong?"

Meg stepped up one more rung on the railing. Even though she was nearly five feet eight inches, she suddenly felt the need of a bit more height advantage. "I wanted you to know that Nikki is in her room and her door is locked."

He shifted the animal closer and his eyes met hers. "You came all the way out here to tell me something I already know?"

Meg fought to keep from pulling away. "No, I didn't just come out here to tell you that. I wanted to ask your permission to take the steps necessary to get her out."

Linc tipped his hat back and wavy black hair fell across his forehead. He leaned against the saddle horn as the horse snorted and danced sideways. "I hired you to do a job. Do it."

Meg's mouth went dry and she had trouble speaking. No man had ever made her feel this jumpy, this nervous. What was the matter with her? "That's all I wanted to know." She leaped down from the railing, sidestepping the horse being led inside, and headed out the wide doorway.

Linc watched Meg walk away. He couldn't miss the gentle sway of her hips, the form-fitting jeans she wore. He shifted in the saddle, feeling the effects her shapely body had on him.

"She's a pretty lady."

Linc glanced down at Dale, noticing that he wasn't immune to Meg Delaney's charms, either. And Linc found he didn't like it.

"Dale, have you picked up Charlie Green's mare?"

"I arranged for Jake to do it this afternoon." The foreman's gaze never wavered from Meg's shapely backside.

Linc felt himself growing angry. "Dammit, Dale. I told you to do it."

Dale placed his hat on his head. "Sorry, boss. I'll take care of it right away." He hurried off.

Linc took one more look at Meg as she disappeared into the house. Damn! He tugged on the reins and turned Devil around to continue working him. He needed to get back to work, too. Meg Delaney had caused him enough distraction for one day.

Linc came through the back door about one o'clock. He was sweaty, dirty and hungry. He pulled off his worn boots and left them on the utility porch, then went into the kitchen. He caught a whiff of Dora's beef stew and his stomach growled. But there was no way she would allow him at the table looking and smelling the way he did. He wrinkled his nose at his soiled clothes.

To the shower, he thought as he walked through the kitchen and into the dining room. He stopped suddenly when he found Meg and Nikki seated at the table. But the real shock came when he saw schoolbooks opened and his sister working on math problems. They glanced up at him.

"Sorry," he apologized. "I didn't mean to disturb you. I'm just headed upstairs."

Nikki dropped her pencil and rushed to him. "Linc, can I stop now?" The teenager glanced over her shoulder at Meg. "She's made me work all day."

Linc raised his hand. "Meg's your tutor. You're supposed to work."

"But she's mean to me."

"I doubt that. Besides, you're the one who got yourself thrown out of school."

"But—"

"I really don't want to hear it," he interrupted. "Meg's

in charge. When she decides you've done enough, then
you can stop working."

"I was planning to break for lunch in a little while,"
Meg offered.

"See, Nik. Meg's not so bad. She's even gonna let you
eat."

Linc winked and watched, intrigued, as Meg shyly lowered her gaze. Most women he'd known would have flirted
back. "If you wait until I shower I'll join you two ladies."

Nikki gave him a pouty look. "Oh, all right."

"Be back in ten minutes," he promised, then headed
for the stairs, climbing them two at a time. Whistling, he
strolled down the hall, tugging his shirt from his pants as
he passed his sister's room. The door was open and he
glanced inside at the chaotic mess. Linc shook his head in
disgust. He needed to get after her about cleaning it.

One thing at a time. Right now, he was just pleased to
see Nikki working with Meg. He went to close the door
and discovered the brass knob was missing. Linc chuckled.
So that's how she got Nikki out.

"Well, I'll be darned. It looks like you may have met
your match, little sister." Linc's smile disappeared as he
thought about the pretty woman who had moved into his
home and into his well-ordered life. "Maybe I have too."

Downstairs, Meg had decided that Nikki Stoner could
give her brothers Rick and Clint lessons in stubbornness.
She glanced toward the cute brunette, remembering the
expression on her face when Meg had removed the knob
from her bedroom door. It was amazing what you could
do with a screwdriver, she thought. Nikki had screamed
for her to get out of her bedroom, and Meg had refused,
of course. Somehow, she'd had to convince the teenager
to get out of bed and take a shower.

Meg had stayed and taken the opportunity to look
around the girl's room. It was incredible. No wonder Nikki

didn't want to leave. Besides the big canopy bed, there was everything a teenager could want, from the latest state-of-the-art stereo system to a television. Even her own phone. The clothes bulging out of the girl's closet hadn't come from the local thrift store, either, nor had the dozen pairs of hand-tooled boots.

Once Nikki had showered, Meg convinced her to come downstairs and have some breakfast. Of course the girl protested, but Meg hung tough until Nikki relented and ate a bowl of cereal and washed it down with a glass of milk. Now, two hours later, Meg discovered that her sister was not only pretty but smart.

"You know, I don't have to do these problems," Nikki said, breaking into Meg's train of thought.

Meg raised an eyebrow.

"I can get my brother to let me have the afternoon off." The teenager smirked.

"Nikki, we've already discussed this."

"No, you told me what I had to do," the girl challenged. "And you're going to put my lock back on my door, too. I need privacy."

"No one is going to come into your room."

"You did."

"That's because you refused to come out and get to work."

"I don't need school."

"What about college?" Meg asked, wanting to shake this child for turning her back on the opportunities open to her.

"Did you go to college?"

"No, but I plan to." Meg sighed, seeing the knowing look on Nikki's face. "As soon as I get settled in Fort Worth. I just don't have the money right now."

"I own half this ranch, so I have a lot of money."

"But it's probably in trust for you until you're twenty-one."

Nikki crossed her arms over her small breasts. "Linc will give me whatever I want."

"Oh, is that so?" came a male voice.

They both turned around to find Linc standing in the doorway. He was fresh from the shower and dressed in a black T-shirt and jeans. His hair was neatly combed and still damp from his shower.

Nikki raced to him and threw her arms around his waist. "Oh, Linc. I'm so glad you're here. I don't feel good. I think I'll go lay down in my room." She started to leave but Linc tugged her back.

"I think you've spent too much time in your room."

"I'm sick."

"Then we'll drive you into town and see the doctor."

Meg was happy to see that Linc was wise to his sister's games. But Nikki didn't give up. She worked hard to produce tears.

"No, I don't want to go see the doctor. I just want to go to my room. My stomach hurts," Nikki insisted.

"Maybe you'll feel better after you eat something," Meg said, fearing that Linc was about to back off.

He brushed back his sister's hair. "Dora made beef stew. It's still your favorite."

Nikki buried her head against his chest. "I can't eat. My stomach hurts too much."

"Okay, maybe you should lay down." He released her and turned her toward the stairs. "I'll check on you later to see how you're feeling."

Meg clenched her fists as she watched the teenager slowly move toward the stairs. She almost wanted to applaud Nikki's performance, but she was too angry.

Linc started for the kitchen. "I think I'll have some lunch. Care to join me?"

Meg followed him to the table.

Linc kissed Dora on the cheek as the woman gave him

a heaping bowl of stew, along with a basket of warm homemade rolls.

"I've died and gone to heaven," he said after he swallowed the first mouthful of food. He glanced at Meg and saw she wasn't eating.

"Don't tell me you're not hungry either."

He waited until she picked up her fork, then dug in again. He was halfway through the bowl before he noticed Meg still hadn't started.

"Is there something wrong?"

"Do you realize that you have undone everything that I accomplished this morning with Nikki?"

"What are you talking about?" he said. "She had a stomachache."

"She was proving to me that she could get her way through you."

"That's crazy."

"We worked for two hours this morning and there wasn't a single complaint until you walked in."

Angry, he dropped his fork. "Are you saying that I should stay the hell out of my own house?"

She glared at him. "No, but you should stay the hell out of my business. This morning you told me to do the job you're paying me to do, then three hours later you stroll in here and let her do whatever she wants."

"All this over a stomachache?"

"It wasn't a stomachache. It was a power struggle between Nikki and me. You let her win, Linc. Now she knows that she can come to you to get her way."

He saw the frustration in her big brown eyes as they met his.

"How am I going to be able to tutor Nikki if I can't discipline her? Remember, you hired me to live here and help supervise her."

Linc had trouble swallowing the lump in his throat. Meg

was right. He had spoiled Nikki all her life. But after all, she was his sister and all they had now was each other.

"All right, you got it. I'll stay out of your way. From now on you handle it." He dropped his napkin on the table and marched out of the room.

Linc didn't stop until he was at Nikki's bedroom door. After knocking twice, he pushed open the door and walked in. To his surprise, his sister was plugged into her headphones, listening to some rock music. He braced his hands on his hips and watched as she danced to the beat. Then she saw him and gasped. She turned off the stereo and removed her headphones.

"I take it you're feeling better?"

Nikki shrugged. "I didn't want to eat with her."

Linc came across the room and grabbed his sister by the arm, making her face him. "I think Mom and Dad would be pretty ashamed of your behavior right now."

She jerked away. "I don't care."

Linc knew that was a lie, but he wasn't going to make an issue out of it. "Come on, you're going downstairs to eat lunch. Then you're going to do schoolwork all afternoon."

"No, I told you, I don't like that woman."

"That woman's name is Meg Delaney. You may call her Meg, or Miss Delaney, but you are never to call her 'that woman' again." He gripped her arms. "Do I make myself clear?"

Nikki looked about to cry, but he wouldn't let that get to him. He would do whatever it took to straighten her out.

Nikki pulled free of his grip. "Yes."

"Okay then, lunch is getting cold." He waited as Nikki walked out of the room and down to the kitchen. Once at the table, she took the seat across from Meg as Dora silently placed a bowl of stew in front of her.

Linc sighed as he picked up his fork. "Now, let's all enjoy our meal."

* * *

Later that evening Meg walked barefoot out to the patio. It was nearly ten o'clock and the house was almost empty. After another silent meal, Linc had left, Dora had gone to visit her sister and Nikki was in her room. Meg had warned the teenager to get a good night's sleep. They would be starting work at eight-thirty sharp.

Meg set her towel on the back of the chair and sat down at the edge of the pool, glad that no one was around to see her faded suit. She twisted the rubber band through her hair, making sure it was in a secure ponytail. She smiled, remembering the awful face Nikki had made at her. It had reminded her so much of her younger brother, Rick. After a few minutes she slid into the cool, refreshing water and began swimming laps, trying to rid her mind of what a disaster her first day as a tutor had been.

Things hadn't gone well. Meg's only hope was that Nikki didn't hate her. She thought back to the promise she had made to her mother. How was she going to fulfill it if Nikki couldn't even stand the sight of her?

Meg's legs kicked harder as her arms sliced through the water, working to reach the end of the pool. Once there, she made her turn and headed back, working off her tension and frustration so she'd be able to sleep. Hopefully by tomorrow she could think of a way to turn things around.

After five laps she was exhausted. She stood in the shallow end, brushing her hair away from her face, when she looked up to find Linc sitting in a chair. "Oh," she gasped. "I didn't know anyone was here."

He leaned forward, bracing his elbows on his knees. He held a long-neck bottle of beer in his hand. "I just got home a few minutes ago." His gaze was on her suit and she had to fight to keep from covering herself.

"I know I should have asked permission to use the pool, but since no one was around…"

"You can use the pool anytime you want, but it's safer if someone is aware that you are out here. What if something happened?"

"I guess I never thought." She began to shiver. It was the cool breeze, she told herself.

Linc couldn't take his eyes off Meg. What a surprise to come out here and find her. The soft pool light acted as a halo around her in the shallow water. His gaze moved to her breasts, seeing her pouty nipples through her thin suit. God! Did she have any idea what she was doing to him?

He stood and grabbed her towel. "Here, you'd better get out before you shake to death." He reached out a hand. She took it and he lifted her effortlessly out of the water. He wanted a closer examination of her long, gorgeous legs, and to see if his hand could span her slim waist, but he quickly resisted the temptation and wrapped the towel around her.

"Thank you," she whispered, and he nearly groaned as he studied her kissable lips. He shook his head.

"I need to thank you for all you're doing for Nikki."

"I haven't accomplished much yet."

"You would have gotten more done without my interfering."

She didn't say anything. Her eyes were so big and dark.

"I don't deny I've spoiled my sister. From the second she came home from the hospital, I wanted to protect her. I wanted to give her everything." He moved away and combed his hand through his hair. "Tell me how to stop."

She smiled at him, and he never realized how sweet a woman's smile was until now. "You don't have to stop, Linc. Just don't let her get out of doing her work. Believe me, she knows exactly what buttons to push with you." Meg grew serious. "I have to talk to Mrs. Simpson tomorrow. She's scheduled an appointment in Fort Worth for Nikki to start her counseling."

"What do you want me to do?"

"Just keep encouraging her."

He nodded, still mesmerized by Meg's sensual mouth. "Anything else?"

"No, I think that's all for now."

That wasn't all for him. He wanted more. He wanted to discover for himself if her mouth was as soft as it looked. Wanted to hold her body against him, feel the warmth of her gentle hand on his skin.

"Just don't give up on my sister."

She smiled again. "I promise I won't."

Chapter Three

He'd had a lousy night.

Linc punched the button on the noisy alarm, then swung his legs over the edge of the bed and sat up. After rubbing his tired eyes, he glanced at the clock and groaned, realizing he'd had only four hours' sleep. He wanted to blame it on the thunderstorm, but it had been his restless mood, caused by one Meg Delaney. Most of the night he kept seeing her standing in the pool, water glistening off her bare shoulders, trickling down between her breasts.

Groaning, he stood and walked to the dresser, grabbed a clean pair of underwear and headed for the bathroom. Dammit! He had to stop thinking about Meg as a woman. She was his sister's tutor, and maybe Nikki's last hope. And what he needed to do was stay out of her way and let her do her job. He stepped into the shower and turned on the faucet, letting the cold spray wake him and shock his aroused body back to reality.

He finished his shower quickly, then dressed in fresh jeans and a Western shirt. He had to drive into Fort Worth today and look at a mare. In stocking feet, he grabbed his black boots and walked down the hall and paused at Nikki's door. A few years ago his sister would have begged him to take her along. Linc smiled, remembering that she had never missed a chance to go to a horse auction. Maybe someday she'll want to go again, he thought as he headed downstairs to breakfast. Following the wonderful aroma coming from the kitchen, he swung open the door, but swallowed the greeting for his favorite cook when he found Meg standing at the stove.

Her blond hair was piled on top of her head, some wayward strands hanging around her sleep-kissed cheeks. His gaze lowered to her light pink-colored T-shirt and faded jeans. Her small feet were bare, creating an air of intimacy in the already warm room. She glanced up at him with that sleepy, tousled look, and he knew his cold shower had been a waste of time.

She smiled. "Good morning."

"Mornin'." He placed his boots on the floor and looked around the kitchen. "Where's Dora?"

"She called a few minutes ago. She's still at her sister's. Her car won't start."

"Does she want me to send someone to get her?" He glanced at the table set for one.

"No, she already had it towed to the garage. Guess you're stuck with me."

"You don't have to fix me breakfast."

Meg removed a strip of bacon from the skillet. "I don't mind. I fed my brothers for years."

He came across the room, buttoning his shirt cuffs. "But that's not what I'm paying you for."

She glanced up at him, but when her large eyes didn't meet his he was disappointed. "It isn't a major problem to fix you some bacon and a few eggs. I'm expecting Nikki for breakfast, anyway."

Linc glanced at his watch, seeing it was only six-thirty.

"I think my sister needs a better reason than schoolwork to get out of bed this early."

"It's not any earlier than she would have to get up for school. Didn't she used to catch the bus about seven-fifteen?"

He nodded.

"Well, I think it's important we keep her on the same schedule."

"You're right," Linc conceded. "But getting her to do it is another story."

She turned the bacon strips. "Nikki needs a routine, Linc. And discipline. I think she's begging for someone to take charge."

Linc went to the coffeemaker and poured himself a cup. He leaned against the counter and sipped the warm brew as he watched his pretty new cook. "I thought I took charge yesterday."

"You did." Meg cracked three eggs onto the griddle. Watching them sizzle a minute, she picked up the spatula and expertly flipped them. Taking a plate from the cupboard, she loaded it with four pieces of bacon, three over-easy eggs and two slices of toast. She set the plate on the table and instructed him to eat, then went to the refrigerator and opened the door. When she bent over to look inside, her jeans pulled taut against her trim bottom. Linc's heart began to race.

Finally she took out a pitcher of orange juice and walked back to the table, noticing he hadn't moved. "Didn't I cook your eggs right? Dora said you liked them over easy."

He quickly pulled out his chair. "No, they're perfect, thank you. But aren't you going to eat?"

She shook her head. "I'll wait." She poured herself a cup of coffee. "What does Nikki like for breakfast?"

He cocked an eyebrow. "Going to try a little bribery?"

Meg saw the twinkle in Linc's eyes as she sank into the

seat at the table. She realized he was teasing her, but if he only knew how hard she had been trying to get a response from Nikki. After yesterday's disaster, Meg was afraid that her sister might already hate her. She sighed, watching as the man across from her dug into his food. "I'm ready to try anything to get her to cooperate so the courts won't take her away. I don't think that a foster home is what Nikki needs."

Linc's fork stopped in midstride. "They'll have to go through me to take her."

Meg cupped her mug. "Your sister is pretty lucky to have you. You're so protective of her. And I'm hoping once we get her back on track with her schoolwork, she'll be ready to accept some counseling to get through this."

Linc reached across the table and touched her arm. "I'm glad you care about her, Meg. I mean, not just as a tutor, but like her friend, maybe even like a sister she can talk to."

The warmth of his large hand seem to be burning her skin. But it was the word *sister* that caused the huge lump in her throat.

"Well, isn't this cozy?"

They both turned toward the doorway to find Nikki standing there smiling. It wasn't a smile as much as a smirk. "Won't Susanne be jealous?"

Linc pulled his hand way and leaned back in his chair. "Good morning to you too, Nikki. You're up early."

The teenager eyed Meg closely. "I wasn't given a choice."

"If you were in school, you'd be waiting for the bus," Linc assured her.

"And I would ditch," Nikki challenged. She started across the room, dressed in a short black skirt that showed too much leg and a bright red top that was too tight. On her feet she wore black boots. Her hair was wild, her pretty face buried under makeup.

Meg glanced at Linc to see that he too wasn't happy about his sister's appearance or her attitude. She had to keep things calm. "How about some breakfast, Nikki?" she asked, getting up.

Nikki walked to the counter. "I'm not hungry. I'll just have coffee."

Linc opened his mouth, but Meg quickly raised her hand to stop his words. "Sure, it'll probably keep you alert so you can do your schoolwork today."

The girl looked confused for a second, then quickly recovered her surprise. "Oh, yeah...sure."

"Sit down and I'll pour you a cup." Nikki did as instructed and Meg filled a mug with strong black coffee. She sure hoped this worked. It had with her brothers. Meg carried the cup to the table and placed it in front of Nikki.

"Why don't you keep your brother company while I go up and shower." She glanced down at her attire, then noticed Linc was staring at her. "Unless you need something else?"

"No, I think we can handle things," he said, and turned to his sister. "Right, Nik?"

"Sure," the teenager answered, doctoring her coffee with a heaping spoonful of sugar.

"Meg." Linc got up and met her in the middle of the kitchen. "I'll be leaving in a little while for Fort Worth. I probably won't be back until late. Most likely I won't be here for supper."

She nodded and had to bite her lip to keep from asking how late.

"Gonna take Susanne with you?" Nikki called from the table.

"I'm taking Dale. We're going to a horse auction," he called over his shoulder. "So you behave today."

"Yeah, sure."

He sighed and rolled his eyes. "Look, Meg, I hate leaving you here alone, but I have to see about this mare."

"It's all right, Linc," Meg assured him. "Nikki and I will be fine. Besides, it will give us time to get to know each other. We'll be busy with schoolwork this morning, and maybe if Nikki makes progress, we'll take off a little early this afternoon."

He smiled and her heart did a flip. "Sounds good. Then I'll see you later tonight."

"Tonight," she echoed, and walked out of the kitchen. She headed upstairs, finding she was actually disappointed that Linc wasn't going to be around today. Then she quickly turned her thoughts to Nikki, knowing she had her work cut out for her.

About one-thirty in the afternoon, Nikki was beginning to fade, so Meg decided it was time to call it a day. They'd already spent four hours that morning, and although they'd only worked an hour after lunch, she was losing the teenager's attention.

Meg shut the geography book. "How about we call it a day?"

"I'm all for that." Nikki got up to leave.

"Wait, you don't have to run off. You want to show me around the ranch?"

The girl stopped. "I want to go to my room and call my friends."

Meg raised an eyebrow. "Aren't your friends in school?"

The girl shrugged. "Then I'll listen to music."

"Why don't we go get some fresh air first?"

Nikki sighed. "Oh, all right." She changed direction and headed for the back door.

Meg quickly followed, anxious to get a good look around. As a little girl, she'd remembered it being the prettiest ranch she'd ever seen. It still was, she thought, as she walked with Nikki through the yard toward the corral area. Of course, back then she had only gotten a glimpse of the beautiful quarter horses from a distance when her daddy had stopped by to talk to Joe Stoner about getting hired on as a trainer.

Then yesterday Meg hadn't been disappointed when she went to the covered arena to find Linc. She had finally gotten a close-up look at the magnificent quarter horses bred on the Stoner Ranch.

Now Meg was excited as a child as she walked up the tree-lined gravel road past the large white-fenced corrals. There were two long barns off to one side. Ranch hands concentrating on their chores were too busy to notice them.

Meg started the conversation as they continued on. "You're pretty lucky to live on a place like this."

"I used to think so when I was younger," Nikki murmured as she stopped at the pasture fence. "Now, I don't like living here anymore."

Meg wanted to take the girl and shake her. Why in God's name wouldn't she want to live here? She had everything she could ever want.

"You know there are a lot of kids who would love to call this home."

"Who?" She climbed up on the fence railing and Meg joined her. The pasture was lush and green and everything smelled of horses and new-mown hay. There was a small herd of horses grazing. Meg couldn't help but admire the beauty of the animals.

"Well, I would have loved it."

"Then you live here," Nikki argued. "I want to live in town with my friends."

"Can't they come out here?"

"Not with my brother always bossing me around. He used to be fun until…"

"Until your parents died," Meg finished, and Nikki turned away. So the girl wasn't as tough as she pretended. "You know that Linc is hurting because of the loss of your parents, too."

"How do you know? You only got here yesterday. You don't know anything." Suddenly Nikki jumped down from the fence and started back toward the house.

Meg quickly grabbed her by the arm. "You're right, Nikki. I don't know anything." There were angry tears in the girl's eyes. "So why don't you tell me?" Nikki tried to pull away. "I know you're hurting because you feel like everyone has deserted you, but that's not true." She watched a mascara-laden tear slide down her sister's cheek. "I want to help you. I want to be your friend." It was true. More than even Meg had realized until that minute.

Meg took a step forward. "Let me be your friend, Nikki." Another tear escaped as Meg drew the resistant girl into her arms. Then Nikki buried her head against Meg's chest and began to cry.

It nearly broke Meg's heart, and she, too, had to fight the tears. Tears for all the years she'd lost not knowing she had a sister. Tears for the pain her mother went through not being able to stand up to her husband and keep her child. But especially for the frightened girl in her arms who felt as if she'd been abandoned.

She soothed Nikki's hair until her crying finally subsided, then the girl stiffened and pulled away. "I want to go to my room."

Meg nodded. "Sure, I think we've both had a long day. Maybe if you feel better later, we can go out for supper."

There was a twinkle of excitement in the girl's eyes, but she quickly masked it. "Don't do me any favors. I'm not sure my brother will pay you overtime." The girl turned and ran off toward the house.

Meg reached out to stop her, but decided it might be best to let her have some time for herself. She needed it, too, recalling how she'd held the sobbing child in her arms. Her sister. All at once it struck her how badly she wanted to tell Nikki that they were related. A tightness circled her heart as she went back to the fence. She climbed up and sat on the top railing, watching as a graceful black mare with a white blaze moved around, her filly following closely on long wobbly legs.

Meg smiled to herself. If only life could be so easy.

About ten that evening Linc stood in the doorway to the patio, watching Meg swim. She was so graceful. She had long slender legs and arms that easily propelled her through the water. He watched as she dove under and her bottom came to the surface. With a groan, he shut his eyes.

Is this what it's come to, he admonished himself, standing in the dark, gawking at an unsuspecting woman? He hadn't done anything like this since he and Jimmy Perkins discovered the peephole to the girls' locker room.

Just then Meg came out of the water. Linc pushed away from the doorjamb and walked toward the pool.

"Hello, Meg," he said when he came into the light.

"Oh, Linc." Her eyes were wide with surprise. "I didn't realize you were here."

"I just got home," he lied "I didn't want to disturb your swim."

"Did you get to see the mare you wanted?" To his disappointment she wrapped the towel around herself.

His gaze raised to her face. "Yeah, I did. In fact, I bought her. As we speak, Josey's Girl is getting used to her new stall."

"That's wonderful."

"If you're interested, I'll introduce you to her tomorrow."

"I'd like that. Nikki started showing me around today—"

"Nikki went out to the barn?" Linc interrupted.

She shook her head, and her wet braid moved against her bare shoulder. "No. We only took a walk out past the corral to the pasture fence. She said she wants to live in town.''

Linc grimaced. ''The new group of kids she has taken up with all live in Mineral Wells. The girls she got in trouble with.'' He shook his head. ''Not two years ago, her best friends were Julie Newton and Cindy James. Both girls come from nice ranching families.''

Meg sighed. ''Well, Nikki has a lot of anger.''

Linc rubbed the bridge of his nose. ''Yeah, well, most of her anger has been directed at me.''

Meg studied Linc Stoner. Even tired with a day's growth of beard, the man was drop-dead handsome. ''You're the closest to her. The only family she has left,'' Meg lied. ''Nikki also knows she can get away with it.''

''What can I say? I guess I'm a pushover for a pretty face.'' A sexy grin appeared as he jammed his hands into his jeans pockets. Was he flirting with her?

Meg glanced away and quickly changed the subject. ''Well, she did work hard today, and I'm hoping tomorrow will even be better.'' She decided not to tell him about Nikki breaking down and crying in her arms. ''I meet with Mrs. Simpson on Friday. I can't wait to see her face when I show her Nikki's progress.''

''I wouldn't mind being there myself.'' He sobered and his eyes searched hers. ''Thank you. I know that Nikki has been a handful.''

His praise made Meg uncomfortable. Not to mention the fact that she was practically naked under her towel. ''Just doing my job.''

Again he flashed her a grin. ''I guess I was pretty rough on you yesterday in the arena.'' He raised a hand. ''I promise it won't happen again. I don't want to come in and find my doorknob missing.''

They both broke into laughter. ''I guess I can be pretty mean with a screwdriver.''

Linc's gaze captured hers once again, causing a warmth

to spread through her body. "Where do you come from, Meg Delaney?" He said her name with a slow Texas drawl.

Meg tried not to show her panic. "Oklahoma." She swallowed. "Boswell, Oklahoma." Oh, please, don't let it be familiar to him.

He moved closer. "What brought you to Texas?"

"I told you my mother passed away a few weeks ago. And since my brothers are old enough to handle the farm, I decided that I needed a change of scenery."

"So you decided to finally leave Boswell and see the world. And you ended up in Mineral Wells?"

Meg shrugged. "I have a friend in Fort Worth I was going to stay with."

"A male or female friend?"

She blinked in surprise. "A female friend."

That seemed to please him. "So you took a little side trip to visit one of your mother's friends."

Fearing he would hear the lie in her voice, she nodded. "I'm glad."

Meg got a rush from his words, even though she knew he was only grateful she was there for Nikki.

"Well, how about I add a fringe benefit and take you riding tomorrow?"

Nikki had been quiet all morning, but she did her algebra problems without argument. She even sat and had lunch, then in the afternoon she began getting restless.

Meg, too, had been distracted most of the day, finding she had been thinking more about Linc than she should. She told herself that she'd just been looking forward to the ride he'd promised her. She checked her watch again. Nearly three o'clock. Oh, well, maybe he forgot, or was too busy.

But then the back door swung open and Linc walked into the kitchen. Her heart raced.

"Well, you two ready to go for a ride?" he asked.

Meg was more than ready, and happy Linc had included Nikki. Her surprise came when the teenager seemed to be pondering the idea.

"I am," Meg answered. "Come on, Nikki, you never finished showing me around yesterday."

"I'm not dressed." The girl glanced down at her short skirt.

"We'll wait. And I'll call down to have Dale saddle up Sweet Sue."

Nikki hesitated and Meg held her breath. "I'll be ready in ten minutes."

Linc nodded and Nikki hurried up to her room. "Take off that makeup so you won't scare the horses," he called after her.

In ten minutes Meg and Nikki had both changed into jeans and boots. Linc grabbed an extra hat off the porch and handed it to Meg. Thanking him, she put it on and they headed across the yard. By the time they were at the corral, one of the hands was leading three saddled horses out of the barn. Meg didn't recognize any of the horses, but Nikki did.

"Oh, Sweetie." She rushed to her chestnut and began petting her muzzle. The filly immediately returned the affection.

Meg and Linc stood back and watched the girl with her horse.

"Sweet Sue's been lookin' for Nikki everyday," Linc said. "My sister's raised her from a colt and they'd been inseparable, until..."

Meg didn't need Linc to finish the thought. She, too, hoped today might start to change things for Nikki.

"This is Josey's Girl." He nodded to the roan. "Think you can ride her?"

Meg's mouth dropped open. "You're going to let me ride your new brood mare?"

"Sure. She needs the exercise. And since you grew up on a farm, I take it you know how to ride."

Meg took the reins from Linc. "Yes, I ride." She eyed the magnificent animal. A few years ago she had made some extra money working with horses, but nothing like the ones on the Stoner Ranch.

Linc climbed on his sorrel gelding and Meg placed her foot in the stirrup and pulled herself up on her mount. Nikki did the same. Linc rode over to the foreman as he came out of the arena and gave him some instructions. When he headed back, Meg's breath caught as he watched how comfortable the man sat in the saddle, how easily he handled the reins. The horse knew instinctively who was the boss.

"I thought we'd head down to Crazy Creek." He looked at his sister. "Is that okay?"

"It makes no difference to me." She still had an attitude, Meg thought, but it was obvious she wanted to be there.

Linc watched as Nikki rode on ahead. She seemed more interested in getting reacquainted with Sweet Sue then conversing with him or Meg. He glanced at the woman beside him. She handled Josey's Girl with ease, but somehow he knew she would. He smiled to himself, remembering how she was practically drooling over the horseflesh when she came into the arena the other day.

"Did you have horses on your farm?"

"We did for a while until my daddy died, then we couldn't afford to keep 'em." She looked at him. "We were pretty busy growing wheat and vegetables. At times we managed a few head of cattle. And since my brothers took over, they're planning on increasing the size of the herd."

Linc realized that his sister's tutor hadn't had an easy time. He knew all about rough times, recalling his own worthless father. "Are you going back to help out?"

She shifted in the saddle. "Probably not. It's time I'm on my own."

"I can't imagine not being here on the ranch. I never realized how much my parents meant to me until it was too late and I lost them. Joe and Pauline took me in when I had nowhere to go. If it hadn't been for them, I don't know what would have happened to me. I don't want Nikki to ever feel that way. I want her to know that she's loved."

Meg put her hand on his arm and whispered his name. "Deep down she does, Linc. She's scared and angry."

They both looked up to see Nikki racing toward the creek ridge. Meg gasped, knowing the girl was going to attempt a jump. It all seemed to happen in slow motion as the horse left the ground and gracefully arched over the creek, landing safely on the other side."

"Dammit," Linc said through clenched teeth. "Nikki, get over here," he called out

With a big smile, Nikki made her way to them. "Didn't she do great? I was afraid that she couldn't handle it—"

"Couldn't is right," he interrupted. "Sue isn't ready for a jump like that. And you haven't been on a horse in months. You could have been thrown and maybe even—"

"Killed?" Nikki finished. She gave her brother a hostile look. "Wouldn't that solve your problem?"

Linc's anger quickly turned to pain. "You're not a problem, Nikki. You're my sister. We're all the family we have left."

The teenager glared at him. "It's your fault. You're the one who killed them," she announced, then jerked the horse's reins and turned her horse. "You killed them." Nikki took off and raced across the pasture.

Linc felt as if his heart had been ripped out.

"Linc, she didn't mean it," Meg assured him. "You're

just the closest target she has and she knows she can hurt you."

He glanced up to see the compassion in her eyes and knew he didn't deserve it. "That's just it. Everything she said is true. It's my fault our parents are dead."

Chapter Four

Linc climbed down from his horse and began to lead the animal across the tall grass. Meg also dismounted, grabbed Josey's reins and hurried up beside him.

"She didn't mean it, Linc."

Silently, he pulled his hat down lower, hiding any expression on his face, and kept on walking.

"Nikki's only angry." Darn that girl. Meg wanted to shake the thirteen-year-old. "She wanted to upset you."

Linc stopped and turned to Meg. His large black eyes were filled with pain. "She was telling the truth."

Josey nudged Meg and she began to rub the horse's neck. "How could Nikki be telling the truth?" she asked, adjusting her hat to shield the sun. "Your parents died in a car crash. You didn't cause the accident."

"I should have been going with my dad to San Antonio. I should have flown him down in the plane," he announced, then marched off. Meg stood there, her mouth gaping, watching as Linc reached a grove of trees and tied his horse on a low branch.

Something occurred to Meg and she hurried after him.

"Wait a minute." She tossed Josey's reins around the same branch. "Do you think it would be better if *you* had died in that crash, too?"

He shrugged. "For Nikki it might have been." He went to the edge of the ravine, watching the stream of water rushing over the smooth rocks. "She could really use a mother right now." He glanced over his shoulder. "As you sure as hell can tell, I'm not exactly doing such a great job. Maybe I ought to let Mrs. Simpson find her a foster home."

"Oh, Linc, you can't mean that. Nikki needs you more than even she realizes. And believe it or not, she loves you."

He squatted down, picked up a rock and tossed it into the water. "And I...I love her." His emotions were obvious in his voice. "But, because of me, she's lost everything."

The muscles in his back flexed with his movement and Meg got an odd sensation in her stomach. "Will you please tell me how you could have prevented your parents' accident."

"I was supposed to fly my dad to the horse auction. But I had made plans to go skiing in Taos."

Meg sat down next to him and picked up a rock. "Did your dad ask you to break your plans and take him?"

He gave her a sideways look. "No. He told me to go on. Said he'd take Mom and they'd just drive down and spend a few days. They have close friends who own a ranch outside town, and they'd stay with them." He shrugged. "They never made it."

Linc studied her for a long time, his eyes revealing his agony. "My dad suffered a heart attack."

Meg tried to hide her surprise as he continued. "Mom was asleep when Dad lost control and veered into an on-coming car. If I'd flown them down I would have been there when Dad had his attack."

"Yes, but who's to say your father would have survived even if...especially if you'd been in the plane?" she stammered, trying to ease some of the guilt he'd been carrying around these past months, with no one at all to comfort him. "You still would have had to land the plane and get him help."

Linc tossed another rock into the creek.

"And can you imagine your mother without your father?" Meg could only think of her own mother and how miserable she'd been during the years after her husband's death. "I never met your parents, but it sounds like they had a special relationship."

He sat down and raised his knee, looking out toward the pasture. "I wasn't really their child. They weren't able to have any. When I was about twelve, I ran away from my old man. I had enough of his whippings. Joe found me in a stall in the barn. I must have looked a sight after three days sleeping with the stock, but he took me to the house, where Pauline cleaned me up and fed me three sandwiches before either one of them asked any questions." Linc paused as a soft breeze rustled through the trees. "They ended up adopting me. Only a week before I turned thirteen." His voice choked. "Pauline was the only mother I ever knew and, Joe was the best. I loved them both."

Meg swallowed hard. "And they loved you, too.

He blinked several times.

"Just as they loved Nikki," she said. "They would never want anything to happen to either of you."

Linc tipped his hat back and sighed. "Joe and Pauline were the kindest and most loving people I've ever met. God, I miss them." He gave her an embarrassed look and forced a laugh. "Here I am nearly thirty and have the responsibility of the ranch and of raising a thirteen-year-old. It scares me to death."

"We're all scared sometimes, Linc."

Suddenly Linc jerked around toward her, seeing the sadness in her eyes. "Christ, Meg. I'm sorry. Here I am crying on your shoulder and you lost your mother only a few weeks ago."

She glanced away, not wanting to add to his sadness. "Our situations are very different."

"She couldn't have been very old. How did she die?"

"Cancer." She still couldn't look at him. "At the end, it was a blessing when she passed on."

Linc's heart went out to Meg. He reached over and stroked his finger down her velvety cheek, then tipped her face up. "That doesn't lessen the pain." Just seeing her eyes misty with tears caused a tightness in his chest. How he wished he could take away her pain. "What about your father?"

Her dark lashes lowered. "He died a long time ago."

"So there's just you and your brothers?"

She nodded, and something compelled him to draw her into his arms. He told himself it was to comfort her, but his body was telling him something different as she buried her face against his chest. He placed his hand against her hair and stroked the long, silky strands. She felt so good in his arms, so soft, so feminine. It had been so long since he had someone to talk to...to care.

He drew back and his gaze dropped to her full mouth, and he was suddenly hungry for a taste of it. Slowly, he leaned closer until his lips touched hers. Just a taste, that was all he wanted. One sweet taste. But one caress proved that there was something happening between them. He raised his head and caught the glint of wonder and excitement in her brown eyes. When she didn't object he went back for more.

Tossing off his hat, he captured her lips in a hungry kiss that left them both breathless. He pulled her against his body and felt a jolt when she accepted the gentle invasion of his tongue.

She made a murmuring sound of pleasure as her arm

moved around his neck. He lowered her onto the cool grass and pressed his aroused body to hers. One kiss faded into another as his hands journeyed over her shapely body. Nothing seemed to exist but her wonderful taste and touch.

Finally he raised his mouth and she whimpered. Her eyes were large and liquid. "I've wanted to kiss you since the first day I found you standing on my porch," he whispered.

Meg froze, suddenly aware of what she had been doing with Linc. Dear Lord! The man was practically on top of her…and his hands were…

She pushed at him until he let her up. She began to straighten her blouse when he reached for her arm. "Meg, what's wrong?"

"Wrong?" She had to clear her throat to get rid of the squeak. "Linc, we shouldn't be doing this. I'm Nikki's tutor." And her sister, she added silently.

He touched her cheek and made her look at him. "That has nothing to do with what just happened here."

"It has everything to do with it. I need to concentrate on helping Nikki." She stood up. Grabbing her hat, she placed it on her head. "Nothing can happen between us."

Trying not to run, she reached Josey and climbed on, then tugged at the reins. Her heels dug into the animal's sides and they took off. Tears blurred her vision as she leaned forward and let the horse run free. The cooling breeze did nothing to ease the heat surging through her body, the heat caused by Linc's gentle touch. She closed her eyes. Oh, Lord! What had she done?

She didn't exactly know, since she hadn't experienced anything like this with any other man. She'd never let anyone touch her like Linc Stoner had. But she felt no shame, only an unbearable aching need for a man she knew she could never have.

Dinner that night was strained, not only between Linc and Meg, but between Nikki and Meg. As much as she tried to keep a conversation going with Nikki, the girl wouldn't respond. Finally Nikki asked if she could go up to her room.

That created another problem—Linc and Meg being alone. She didn't want to deal with that, either. As much as she wanted to be in the man's arms, she knew she couldn't let it happen again. So she, too, excused herself and spent the evening in her room.

There, Meg found things to do. She wrote her brothers a letter and told them about her job. Of course, they didn't know about Nikki yet. When Nina Delaney confessed about the baby she'd given up, Meg wanted to check the story out before telling anyone. As far as Clint and Rick were concerned, she had a tutoring job outside of Fort Worth.

A flash of lightning suddenly lit up the dark sky, and Meg walked to the window. She pulled back the curtain as a cool breeze rushed against her face. There was a storm moving in. She glanced down and discovered the patio lights were on. That wasn't all she found. Linc was in the pool.

Her breath caught as she watched him swimming tirelessly, finishing one lap, then turning and starting another, his long arms and legs slicing through the water with ease. She pressed her hands against the cool pane, recalling the feel of Linc's body against hers.

Another flash of lightning and Meg tensed, reminded of the coming storm. He shouldn't be in the water. Her gaze returned to the figure in the pool. She was relieved that Linc was coming up the steps at the shallow end. But seeing his fitted nylon suit didn't help slow her heart rate any.

The man was gorgeous. Meg felt heat creep up her body as her hungry gaze slid over his broad chest and long muscular legs—chest and legs that had been pressed against her just hours ago.

She dropped the curtain and hurried back to her bed. She had to stop thinking about him. With the situation the way it was, she couldn't allow herself to fall for Linc Stoner. She had to think about Nikki, about their visit to the counselor tomorrow. About getting the girl's life straightened out, getting her back in school. Then Meg's job would be done.

She could go on with her life and Linc and Nikki Stoner could go on with theirs. Without her.

"Well, how did you like Dr. Hamilton?" Meg asked as she took her eyes off the highway for a second.

Nikki shrugged. "She wasn't too bad. She didn't make me talk about anything I didn't want to. And I get to call her Kathy."

"So you're not upset about going back next week?"

The girl shrugged. "Like I said, she's not too bad."

Meg smiled, noticing that Nikki had on less makeup today and her skirt was a little longer. "Believe it or not, Mrs. Simpson was the one who recommended her."

Nikki looked surprised. "That old witch?"

"Nikki, that's not a nice thing to say." They exchanged glances and laughter. It felt good. "What do you think about staying in town to have lunch?"

"And maybe go shopping?"

Meg sobered, thinking about the forty dollars she had in her wallet. "Well, we didn't bring any money."

Nikki dug into her purse and pulled out a credit card. "I did."

Meg's mouth dropped open and she glanced back to the road. "Where did you get that?"

"Linc gave it to me," she admitted. "He hates shopping so he drops me at the mall and hands me a card."

That explained the girl's strange outfits, Meg thought.

She needed to talk to Linc about someone supervising his sister's purchases. "Well, summer is coming. Maybe it won't hurt to call and ask Linc for permission."

Once again Nikki reached into her purse, this time pulling out a fold-up cellular phone.

"Where did you get that?" Meg asked, then answered her own question. "Linc."

Nikki finished punching in the numbers and held it to her ear. "Linc," she began. "Meg and I just finished at the doctor's and— Yeah, it was okay. Yeah, hold on." The girl held out the small black device. "He wants to talk to you."

Meg wasn't sure what to do. She had never had to drive and talk on a phone at the same time. She placed it against her ear. "Hello."

"Meg." Linc's deep voice rang out from the earpiece. "How did it go?"

"Pretty good. I'll tell you about it later." She glanced at her passenger. "Nikki wants to know if it's okay to stop for lunch and maybe go shopping."

"I think it's a great idea. That is, if it's not too much trouble for you."

"I don't mind at all. And Nikki seems to have a credit card that you gave her."

"Yeah, let her get whatever she wants."

Meg eyed the girl, who was playing with the dials on the radio of her old car. "I'm not sure that's a good idea, Linc. Her buying habits could use a little supervision."

"Oh, yeah, you're probably right," he agreed. "Do you think you can help her?"

"I'll see that everything gets covered. We'll try not to be too late." She started to give the phone back to Nikki when Linc lowered his voice and added.

"Thanks, Meg, for everything. And hurry home. I miss you both."

She felt the blush rise to her cheeks as Nikki looked at her. "Bye, Linc," Meg said.

"Is something wrong?" Nikki asked.

Meg wished her car had air-conditioning. "No, just tell me where to go. We'll have the rest of the day to shop."

"All right," Nikki crowed.

Meg was excited, too, but not by the idea of spending the day shopping with a thirteen-year-old. It was Linc's waiting for her to return to the ranch. A man she had no business thinking about as anything other than her employer. A man who was off-limits.

Meg strolled out to the patio that evening. She hadn't been able to swim the past few days and she was really looking forward to it tonight. She set her towel on the chair, walked to the edge of the pool and dove in. The shock of the cool water disappeared as she surfaced and started swimming. But after a few more laps she suddenly sensed she wasn't alone.

Meg came up at the deep end and discovered Linc had joined her. Her pulse raced and the ache in her stomach intensified as she watched the man slip effortlessly into the pool. For the past week she had tried to avoid him. Keeping her distance seemed to be the smartest and safest way to stay away from temptation.

He definitely wasn't helping. She watched in near panic as he swam toward her.

He surfaced wiped the water from his face and tossed her a breathless "Hi."

"Hi, Linc." She, too, had trouble drawing air into her lungs as he moved closer. He braced his arms on either side of her head.

"I've missed you."

"I've been busy. Nikki and I had a lot of work to do."

"I know, I've talked with her."

"Is she complaining?"

"Not hardly. She seems excited lately. More than I've seen her in a long time. You're working wonders with her."

"It's not as hard as you think. I've just spent time with her and...and we talk."

He tensed. "Are you saying that I'm not giving her enough attention?"

"I'm suggesting you sit her down and talk to her about your feelings."

He glanced away. "She knows I love her."

"Spoiling her isn't sharing your feelings."

He shot her an angry look, then it softened. He reached out and brushed the hair off her forehead and smiled. "But I like to spoil my women."

"But there's good spoiling and bad spoiling."

He leaned forward, and she could feel his breath on her face. "What kind do you like, Meg?" His finger traced her lips and she gasped at the sensation. "Do you want me to be good or bad?" He leaned closer and she closed her eyes as his mouth took hers in a gentle but persuasive kiss. Everything seemed to be spinning and her insides quivered.

Below the water, his body pressed against hers, their bare legs tangled, sending an unbelievable sensation to her very core. His arm gripped her waist as his mouth continued to feed on hers. Then he pulled away and looked into her eyes. Something urgent, something undeniable was happening between them and Meg couldn't seem to stop it.

He took her mouth again. This time she eagerly returned the kiss, releasing a groan as his tongue found hers, then flicked against the roof of her mouth. She moaned and his hand tracked up her ribs until he reached her breasts.

"Linc..." she whispered.

"Meg, I need to touch you," he told her. His hand

tugged at the strap on her suit as his lips placed kisses along her neck.

Between them they somehow managed to dispense with the strap. Linc lowered her suit just below the water. "Oh, Meg. You're gorgeous." His eyes met hers with a smile. Then he lifted her slightly and took the tip of her breast into his mouth. Her eyes closed and she was lost in the powerful feeling this man evoked in her. A small cry escaped her lips. Linc's mouth closed over hers and her arms circled his neck. They were suddenly moving. She broke off the kiss to discover she was lying on top of him and he was swimming on his back, taking them toward the shallow end.

"I need two hands." He tossed her a sexy grin and stood, pulling her up with him. Suddenly cool air brushed against her skin, quickly bringing her back to reality. Embarrassed, she covered her nakedness.

"Don't be shy." Linc moved toward her. "Your body is beautiful." He kissed her neck and she pulled away.

"I can't do this." She began to tremble. "I work for you."

Linc searched her face, seeing her panic. God, he'd never wanted a woman so badly. "That can't change what's happening between us."

"But we've known each other less than two weeks." She glanced around. "It's happening too fast."

He raised a calming hand. "Okay, okay, we'll take it slow."

"No!" She moved away. "We can't even let it happen."

Was she saying never? "Look, Meg, you can't deny we're attracted to each other. We were both doing a pretty good job of heating up the pool."

"I don't go to bed with men just because there's an attraction." She headed for the steps and climbed out, and he followed.

"I know that, Meg." He handed her a towel. She wrapped it around herself, but it didn't stop her shaking. The urge to pull her back into his arms was so strong he clenched his hands into fists. "Look, I want to make love to you, but I would never force you."

She avoided his gaze. "I don't want to talk about it. I just want you to leave me alone so I can do my job." She turned on her heel, walking across the patio and into the house.

Linc had to fight with himself not to run after her. He knew Meg wanted him just as much as he wanted her. She had returned his kisses, his touches. His body stirred to life once again. He raised his eyes to her bedroom window, seeing her light go on.

"Meg Delaney, you're going to find out I don't give up so easily."

Chapter Five

One day after lunch, Meg walked out the back door and headed toward the horse arena. It was nearly two o'clock and she'd just gotten back from a conference with Nikki's teachers and school principal. They all seemed to be pleased with her sister's progress and the fact that she'd been to counseling. Meg also got the lesson plans for the next few weeks and optimistic words about Nikki's return to class.

Meg felt somewhat relieved herself, despite wondering if she was giving her sister what she needed. She wasn't a professional, but somehow she seemed to be getting the girl on track. But would Nikki stay there?

What about when Meg had to leave? And as much as she wanted to avoid it, she knew she couldn't stay indefinitely. Her thoughts turned to Linc, remembering the kisses they'd shared by the creek and in the pool. Heat rose to Meg's face as she drew in a sharp breath. She could still feel his mouth against hers, his hands on her... Never in her life had she dreamed she would have these feelings, especially not after the humiliating life her mother went through because of a man.

She shook her head. She shouldn't be having those feelings, either. As much as Meg might want to, she couldn't stay at the ranch. If Nikki found out about their being related, it might devastate the girl. And Meg cared too much about her sister to let that happen. Sadly, for now, all she could be to Nicole Stoner was her tutor and friend.

Meg reached the arena and walked inside, hoping to find Nikki. Over the past week, she suspected the thirteen-year-old had been spending time in the vicinity of Sweet Sue. Dale had reported that Nikki had been hanging around the two-year-old chestnut's stall. Of course, she had made excuses that she was looking for her brother. Meg was happy that Nikki was taking an interest in her horse again.

During their trips into Fort Worth twice a week for counseling sessions, Kathy had assured Meg that Nikki was opening up. The doctor asked that Linc call and set up an appointment to see her so they could eventually come in together as a family.

Meg figured it was going to be a long time before she could get Linc anywhere close to seeing a "shrink," as he called the doctor. It saddened Meg, because she thought that problems lay between Nikki and Linc.

If they only realized how important they were to each other. Although it was breaking her heart, Meg knew. She had come to love them both, and they would never know. Maybe in a few years she could come back and tell Nikki, but Linc—

"Hey, stranger, what are you doing out here?"

Meg jerked around to find Dale. "Oh, I was looking for Nikki. I just got back and we need to get started on her geography lesson."

The foreman frowned. "That doesn't sound like much fun." He motioned for her to follow him and they walked through the doors to an outside corral. To her surprise they found Nikki on Sweet Sue's back, busy working her horse. Meg folded her arms over her chest, intrigued, watching the young girl in worn jeans, a battered Stetson cocked on her head, pulling her chestnut through reining training. It might have been months since Nikki worked out with Sweet Sue, but it was obvious there was a special bond between them. And how easily, how confidently, Nikki sat in the saddle and worked her horse.

Meg felt tears sting her eyes. Daddy would have been proud of his youngest daughter.

"She's a natural," Dale said.

"She is good."

"Linc has worked with Nikki since she could barely walk. Used to drive Mrs. Stoner crazy, too. She was so afraid her daughter would get injured." Dale shook his head. "But Linc would never let anything happen to Nik." The foreman sighed. "He'd give his life for that girl."

Linc walked out of the barn and spotted Dale talking with Meg. His heart suddenly went into overdrive, as it had every time he saw her. Although that had been very little the past week. Ever since they'd gone riding and he kissed her, she'd done everything possible to avoid him. And it only got worse after the pool incident.

Laughter rang out between his foreman and Meg, and Linc didn't like it. He moved out of the shadows.

"What's so funny?" he asked, noticing the uncomfortable look on Meg's face.

"Just telling Meg the story about Blackie," the foreman answered.

"Yeah, old Blackie was quite a character," Linc agreed, never taking his eyes off Meg. She was dressed in a dark skirt and prim-looking white blouse that showed off the fact that his presence was causing her to breathe rapidly.

His gaze went to her mouth, remembering how sweet she tasted. "Blackie stood in stud around here for nearly twenty years."

Dale shook his head. "A lot of our brood mares were pretty sad when he passed away a few years back. Blackie sure knew how to keep them happy."

Meg looked toward the corral. "More men should learn."

Linc exchanged a quick glance with Dale, and the foreman grinned. "Well, I better get back to work." He started to walk off. "Meg, if you ever get bored and need a workout, come looking for me. I'll let you exercise some of the horses."

"I'd like that," she answered with a smile. "Thanks."

Well, Linc didn't like it. If anyone was going to take her riding, he was. "You know you can ride anytime."

Meg shaded her eyes as she looked up at him. "You wouldn't mind?"

"Of course not," he said, and nodded toward the corral. "I think Nikki would like some company." He sighed. "She sure looks happy. But she always did when she was on a horse." He turned back to Meg. "I don't want to talk about Nikki. I want to talk about us. Why have you been avoiding me?"

"I told you before, Linc. I can't let anything interfere with my job. What would Nikki think?"

"Yeah, what about her? Do you think that it would devastate her if we decide to date? I've dated before."

Meg's temper flared. "No doubt. But I think you should be thinking about Nikki right now." She was breathing hard, and she knew it wasn't because of her anger. If only she could tell Linc the truth. No! He might throw her off the ranch. And he'd have a perfect right. The Delaneys had lost all rights to Nikki when her father signed the adoption papers.

"I'm only going to be staying for a short time. We shouldn't start anything that..." She glanced away. It hurt too much to look at him.

Suddenly he gripped her arm, pulled her into the barn

and into the corner of an empty stall. "It's a little late to think about approaching this cautiously. You want me as much as I want you and I can prove it." Before she could protest, he jerked her against his body and his mouth came down on hers in a searing kiss.

All Meg could do was grasp his shoulders as her mouth yielded to his, opening eagerly when his tongue demanded entrance, then stroked and caressed hers until she could only want more. Her arms circled his neck and she pressed closer to him, inhaling the wonderful scent of his soap and leather. She felt her pulse pounding in her ears as his mouth threatened to set her body aflame. She whimpered as he moved to her breasts, his hands kneading them until her nipples grew hard against his palm.

Suddenly the sound of men walking by outside caused her to jerk away. Linc refused to release her, though. He held her close until the men were gone, then kissed her on the end of the nose and released her. "I guess we should find a more private place."

Meg took a long, slow breath. "We're not going to find anything."

He tossed her a narrow look. "Come on, Meg. Don't try and tell me there isn't something between us."

Meg brushed her hair away from her face. "That doesn't mean we have to act on those feelings."

"I don't see why not."

"Because we have to think about Nikki."

He looked frustrated. "Why don't we ask her if she minds us being together?"

She grabbed his arm to stop him. "No!"

He stared at her.

"Don't you see that I don't want to start something with you." It was a lie, but she wouldn't allow herself to get into a situation like her mother's. No matter how much she cared for the man. "I'll be gone in a few weeks."

"But only to Fort Worth," he answered. "It's only

thirty miles away. You can't give up on us, Meg," he urged. "You can't throw away what's happening between us without giving it a chance."

She shook her head. Her own fears held her back from answering the truth. "I can't, Linc. Nikki has to be my only concern right now. I talked with her teachers today and they agreed that she's doing so well that as soon as the counselor gives the okay, she'll be able to go back to school. That reminds me, Dr. Hamilton would like to set up a session with you and Nikki together."

He jerked off his hat and smacked it against his thigh. "Hell, the last thing I need is a shrink digging into my business." He started to walk away and Meg stopped him.

"Linc." She gripped his arm. "I wouldn't ask if it wasn't important."

His dark gaze searched her face. Meg wanted nothing more than to go back into his arms, forget all her fears and let this man take her to heaven. She swallowed. "Please, Linc."

He closed his eyes with a long sigh. "I guess you don't leave me much choice." He looked down at her hand on his arm; it was trembling. "Don't think I'm giving up, because I'm not." He raised his hand. "But first we'll concentrate on Nikki."

Late afternoon Linc and Nikki came out of Dr. Hamilton's office, rode down the elevator and walked through the parking garage without a single word spoken. He unlocked the doors of his truck, climbed inside, but didn't start the engine.

He lay back against the headrest and closed his eyes. For the past two hours he had spilled his guts in hopes of helping his sister.

"Are you ever going to speak to me?" He stared straight ahead. Too many things had been said not to talk about it. He knew Nikki hated him, but that didn't change the fact that he was going to be her guardian until she turned eighteen. So they had to find a way to get along. Her silent treatment wasn't cutting it.

"Oh, Linc." Her voice was raw with emotion. "I never knew your daddy used to beat you."

Linc gripped the steering wheel, hating the fact she had to find out. "It doesn't matter, it was a long time ago."

"But he hurt you."

"Yeah, it hurt." Linc could still feel the pain sometimes, especially since the death of the Stoners. "But then Joe saw to it that my daddy couldn't get to me anymore."

He looked at the pretty dark-haired girl he'd loved since the day she came home when she'd been two days old. She had tears in her eyes. "It was a long time ago, Nik."

She shook her head. "But I never knew. I thought your parents died."

"That's what I wanted you to think. When my old man died I wanted my past buried with him. Barely anyone around here remembers old Ben Norris. Joe made sure of that. And by the time you arrived," he said with a smile, "I was Joe Stoner's kid." He reached across the seat and touched her small hand. "Just as you were."

Her pretty heart-shaped face showed confusion. "But at least you knew where you came from." Her blue eyes looked questioningly at him. "I don't."

Linc tried not to get angry. "Trust me, you really don't want to know. My mom didn't love me. She ran off with another man and left me with a father that waited for me to do something wrong so he'd have an excuse to slap me around." He squeezed her hand. "Just count yourself lucky that your mother gave you up so you'd have a better life with the Stoners."

More tears flooded her eyes. "But they're gone."

He drew a long breath and brushed the moisture from her cheek. "I know it's not the same, Nik, but you have me. And I'm not going anywhere."

"You promise?"

Linc knew she was afraid of something happening to him, like their parents. "There have been days I might have wanted to give you away, but..." He shrugged. "It would probably get pretty lonely around here. And I'm expecting you to hang around so when you get a little older, you can help me run the ranch."

Nikki turned in the seat, excitement twinkling in her blue eyes. "You really mean it?

He nodded. "It's all in Dad's will. We're equal partners."

"What about when you get married?"

Linc's thoughts immediately went to Meg. It threw him that she'd been the only woman he'd even given any thought of settling down with. But she'd put up so many roadblocks. "I don't think you have to worry about that. When the eligible females in Mineral Wells find out I'm stuck with a bratty kid, they'll keep their distance. You'll probably be taking care of me in my old age."

Nikki punched her brother in the arm. "That's not funny. Don't you see Susanne anymore?"

He shook his head. Six months ago Susanne showed her true colors when she wanted him to get rid of Nikki. "I don't think she was as interested in me as in the Stoner Ranch and the money."

"I'm sorry," Nikki said, lowering her eyes. "I know I didn't help matters any with all the problems I caused."

"Let's say you helped me discover the real woman."

She smiled. "I'm glad then. I never liked her."

"Brat." He reached over and tweaked her nose. She began to giggle and Linc had never heard such a sweet sound. He pulled his sister into his arms and gave her a big hug. They had a long way to go, but things were starting to look a lot better.

Meg had been staring out the living room window until it was too dark to see anymore. Where were they? she wondered. Linc and Nikki had been gone all afternoon and missed dinner. Dora hadn't seemed surprised or worried at all.

They need to spend time together, the housekeeper had said. And it's about time they worked out their problems. Meg couldn't have agreed more, but why weren't they home?

Finally she saw the headlights of Linc's truck pull into the driveway and circle around to the back of the house. She rushed into the kitchen, then stood by the table and tried to act calm as the two came through the door. Their laughing voices rang out as the brother and sister strolled in.

They stopped and sobered on seeing her. Meg almost felt hurt. "Looks like you two had a nice afternoon."

"Oh, Meg, it was great. After seeing Dr. Kathy, Linc took me out to dinner to my favorite pizza place." She glanced at her watch. "I know it's late, Meg, but I promise I'll be up early in the morning for our lessons."

Meg's gaze shifted between Nikki and Linc. "It's okay, Nikki. You're allowed to go out with your brother." She smiled. "Sounds like you had a lot to celebrate."

"Just that I've been a brat." Nikki glanced at Linc. "And that I should count my blessings." She hugged him and placed a kiss on his cheek. "Good night, Linc. Thanks for being there."

He looked unconvinced. "Until the next time I have to tell you no."

Nikki batted her eyes. "You were always an easy mark. Night, Meg."

"See you tomorrow, Nikki," Meg answered as the girl hurried out of the room.

Meg's attention turned to Linc as he leaned against the counter and crossed one shiny-booted foot over the other. His black jeans pulled taut against his thighs and flat stomach. Her pulse began to race as she continued her journey over the starched white shirt fitted over his broad shoulders. There was no air left in her lungs as her gaze reached his handsome face. Suddenly he winked at her.

Oh, Lord! He had caught her. She glanced away. "Well, it seems like the two of you made some headway today."

Linc smiled to himself. As much as Meg Delaney wanted to deny it, she was interested in him. "Yeah, Nik and I did a lot of talking." He pushed away from the counter and came toward her. "I think we've solved our problem."

"I like your optimism," Meg said. "I'm sure Dr. Hamilton will be happy to hear of your progress."

"Good, you call and tell her." Linc knew he wasn't going to spend another minute in that shrink's office.

Meg frowned. "But you're going back."

He shook his head. "I can't see what more I can do to help. Nik and I are getting along just fine now." He raised his hand to her face, touching her soft cheek. He inhaled her sweet fragrance and it drove him half-crazy. "So that leaves enough time to concentrate on us."

"There is no 'us.'" Meg stepped back and began walking around the kitchen. "Nikki needs you, Linc. You can't be a part-time parent."

"And I'm gonna be here for her," he explained, a little angry she didn't think he took his responsibility seriously. "And she's promised that she'll come to me and tell me when I screw up. We even talked about starting her back in the quarter horse shows. After summer school is finished, we're going to get Sweet Sue and her ready for competition."

"I think that's wonderful," Meg agreed. "But Dr. Hamilton feels that Nikki needs to stay in therapy for a while longer."

"And I feel the same," Linc said. "But I'm finished

baring my soul." He raised a hand to stop her protest. "That's all."

Meg clenched her fists. The man was stubborn as a mule. She could see that she wasn't going to get through to him. She squared her shoulders. "If that's the way you feel, I guess there's nothing more to say." She started across the room, but he grabbed her by the arm, nearly spinning her around to face him.

"There is plenty left to say. This, for starters." He lowered his head and slanted his mouth over hers, smothering any further protest she might have.

Meg was dying a slow, passionate death. The man's lips were lethal. By the time he released her, she was swaying and nearly unable to stand up.

Linc wrapped his arms around her protectively and whispered, "How about we put on our suits and continue this discussion out by the pool?"

Meg's eyes darted open. She was doing it again! She was going to let him... "I can't," she said, and fought to pull away. "Linc, please. You're not making this easy for me."

"For you? What about me?" He jerked her up against him, making it obvious the effect she had on him. "I want you, Meg Delaney, until I think I'm going crazy. I know I've chased you around these past few weeks like a randy high school kid. There's a difference, though. I'm not a kid, and I'm not after a one-night stand."

Meg managed to swallow but couldn't speak.

"I think we could have something special, if only you'd give it a chance."

So many things were flooding Meg's head. She wanted to trust him. Would he feel the same if he knew who she really was? She had lied since her arrival at the Stoner Ranch. There were so many things that stood between them. But, God help her, she wanted to believe him.

"I'm scared."

He closed his eyes and leaned his head against hers. "Like I'm not? I promise, Meg, I won't ask for more than you're willing to give."

It all sounded so wonderful, just like a fairy tale. "But, Nikki—"

"We won't interfere with Nikki. I just want to spend some time with you, even if it's just an hour sitting out on the patio or swimming in the pool."

Meg stiffened, remembering how quickly things got out of hand last time. "Maybe we should stay away from the pool for a while."

"Chicken," he said, a teasing glint in his eyes.

She felt her cheeks flush. "Just sensible. There is a teenager in the house. We need to set an example."

He released her. "Okay, you make the ground rules, Meg. I just want us to spend time together. How about tomorrow afternoon we go riding?"

Meg bit her lip to keep from answering too anxiously. "What about Nikki's lesson?"

"I thought afterward," he answered. "I'll be gone most of the day anyway. How about three or four? We'll have plenty of daylight. Besides, Nikki mentioned she was thinking about calling her old friend, Julie Newton. If we're lucky they'll spend hours on the phone catching up on news."

Meg tried to hold back a smile as excitement raced through her. "Hours, at least," she agreed.

"So, you'll meet me at the back corral at about three-thirty tomorrow?"

It felt like her heart was about to drum itself right out of her chest as he leaned toward her. Her good sense told her to push him away, make him keep his distance. Instead, she closed her eyes as his mouth caressed hers. As she yielded to him, as her arms circled his neck and she pressed against him, hot desire consumed her body. Her need for Linc was so intense, she was unaware when he broke off the kiss and lifted her arms from his neck.

He drew a long breath. "We better slow down or we're going to start a fire right here in the kitchen."

Embarrassed, Meg lowered her head. Her hands covered her face. "I'm sorry."

Linc tipped her chin up to meet his gaze. "I'm not. But I promised you slow and easy, and that's what I'm gonna give you." He raised her hand to his mouth and placed a soft kiss on the palm. "Good night, Ms. Delaney," he said with a flourish. "I look forward to seeing you tomorrow." He turned and walked out, leaving Meg weak-kneed and confused.

Meg went to the table and collapsed in a chair. "Oh, Mama, what have I gone and done?"

The next afternoon, Devil danced away from the corral gate as Linc tugged on the horse's reins. "Whoa, boy." He coaxed the restless stallion back under control. But he knew it wouldn't last. The powerful animal snorted his irritation and scraped his hoof against the hard dirt. Linc used a stern, no-nonsense voice to try to calm him.

The priceless stud suddenly reared up, but Linc held on tight, allowing the animal to circle the corral. Was riding Devil today such a good idea? he wondered. The horse needed exercising, but he didn't want to end up on the seat of his pants.

"You old bag of bones, behave." He once again got the animal under control.

"You need some help?"

Linc glanced up to see Meg coming through the gate. She was dressed in a white blouse, a pair of faded jeans and scuffed brown boots. Perched on her head was a battered cowboy hat from the rack by the kitchen door. She looked adorable.

"Be careful. Prince Charming here isn't being very sociable." He glanced over his shoulder and yelled to one of his men to saddle up another horse, his words trailing off as he watched Meg approach Devil without any fear. Her voice was soft and just a little seductive as she drew the animal's attention.

"What's the matter, boy," she said huskily. "Aren't you getting your way?"

Devil stopped and eyed her curiously, then made a snorting sound. Meg reached for his halter, holding him firmly as he bobbed his head. To Linc's surprise, she raised her hand and stroked the horse's muzzle. Soon the animal calmed down.

"I guess he just wants a little attention," she said.

Linc's body came to life as he watched her run her long fingers over the animal's neck. He was suddenly envious of the horse. He swung his leg over the saddle and jumped down. "What this guy wants can only be helped by a seasoned brood mare. I was hoping a good hard ride would settle him down a little."

Devil again shifted nervously and Linc had had enough. He grabbed the reins. "Sorry, fella, but I'm not gonna let you wreck a perfect afternoon with my girl because you can't control your urges."

Meg's gaze shot to Linc. His girl? She stared at the gorgeous man in the chambray shirt and faded jeans. He pushed his familiar Stetson off his forehead and winked. She felt her face redden and her insides stir. She glanced away. "Where are we going?"

"I thought I'd take you to the north section and show you some of our scenery. We have a great view of the river."

A hand came out of the barn, leading two horses. One was Josey's Girl, the other the sorrel gelding Linc had ridden the other day. Linc made the exchange with the trainer and brought the two docile animals to Meg.

"Here." He put the reins in her hand. "You remember Josey."

Meg rubbed the roan's head. "How are you, girl?"

"This guy's full name is Ace in the Hole. Dad gave him to me when I graduated from high school. We just call him Ace."

Linc dropped Ace's reins and walked to Meg to help her mount. She placed her booted foot in the stirrup as he put his hands on her waist. His touch suddenly made her weak, and she almost didn't make it into the saddle. Once settled, Linc took the time to adjust her stirrups, before finally going back to his horse.

"You ready?" he asked.

Meg's heart was racing as she answered, "Yes." She had always felt exhilarated when she got on a horse.

One of the men opened the corral gate, and Linc motioned for her to go first. Josey nickered, anxious to get going, too. Meg had to hold her back as they rode past the outer buildings and toward the trail that led to the creek.

"I thought we could head up the ridge." He rested his palms against the saddle horn and nodded off in the distance, toward the rich green rolling hills.

Meg nodded.

Linc guided Ace next to her mare and suggested, "How about givin' these guys a little exercise first?"

Meg caught his mischievous grin. "Sounds good."

"Then I'll see you at the creek." With his grin intact, he kicked his horse's sides and took off.

Meg took the challenge without hesitation as she nudged Josey into a gallop. "Not if you see me there first," she called as she raced by him.

Linc's mouth dropped open as he heard her laughter and watched her beautiful blond hair flying wildly from beneath her hat.

"Come on, Ace, we can't let the ladies show us up." He leaned forward and coaxed the animal on. Coming up behind them, Linc discovered he was more interested in the curve of Meg's thighs pressed tight against the horse's sides, and the taut pull of her jeans hugging her trim bottom, than in winning the race.

Linc drew a needed breath, wondering if today's ride was a good idea. He promised to keep his hands off Meg, but every time he got close to her he couldn't think of anything else.

Luckily Ace had his attention on the race and moved ahead to nose out the mare at the last minute. Linc slowed his horse and came back to Meg. He climbed off and held her reins as she swung her leg over Josey and jumped down.

"In a fair race, I could probably beat you," she announced.

Linc laughed. "When I'm old and gray."

Meg raised an eyebrow. "We'll see."

Together they led the animals to the creek for a drink, then mounted and continued toward the ridge. This time they went at a much slower pace, taking time to enjoy the scenery.

Meg loved hearing Linc talk about the ranch. He had such pride in his voice as he spoke about his family.

"The Stoners have been here for four generations. When Joe lost his younger brother in Vietnam, the ranch nearly went under."

Linc led the way around the thorny mesquite trees as the trail narrowed down, but Meg stayed close, eager to hear more of the story.

"How did things get turned around?"

"Pauline came into Joe's life. Actually, it was Pauline and a quarter horse stud named Blackie. Back twenty-five years ago, the Stoners raised cattle, but with beef prices always fluctuating, and drought and disease, they couldn't seem to get ahead. Joe had always bred horses on the side, then branched out into training. He was surprised by the demand for good saddle horses.''

Linc reached the top of the ridge and waited for her to join him. He drew a deep breath and asked, ''Well, what do you think of the view?''

Meg's gaze couldn't move fast enough to take it all in. Large trees lined the ridge as if to guard the lush green valley below. A soft breeze rustled the leaves and brushed against her cheeks like a caress. Her eyes lowered to the river that divided the land. Along its bank she caught sight of a doe taking a drink.

''Oh, Linc, it's beautiful.'' She got off Josey.

''I used to come here a lot when I first lived with Joe and Pauline.'' He, too, dismounted, then pulled off his hat and wiped his forehead. ''I guess I had a lot of trouble adjusting.'' He seemed to be lost in thought, then suddenly pointed through the trees. ''See down there.''

Meg searched until she found what he was talking about. ''It's a cabin.''

''Yeah, Dad and I built it. It took us about a month. It's pretty rustic. You have to pump water from a well, and there aren't any proper bathroom facilities, but it was my favorite place in my teen years. Dad said sometimes a man needs to be alone. He came here, too, and we'd talked for hours.'' Linc shrugged. ''Well, Joe would talk. Back then I was pretty withdrawn. He'd tell me about things, anything from old Indian stories about the *palo pinto,* the spotted trees—'' he pointed to the oak ''—to how he and Pauline met.''

There was silence for a long time. Then he turned toward her, looking embarrassed. ''Sorry. It's just that I haven't come here since…for a long time.''

Meg saw his pain and knew how much he missed his parents. She couldn't find the words. Instead she went into his arms.

Linc loved the feel of Meg's body against his. It was

heaven. He suddenly stiffened. How could he keep his promise with her draped all over him?

"It's okay." He placed his hands on her back and fought off a groan as he felt her warm breath against his chest. He finally managed to pull away. "Maybe we should head back, before someone starts to worry about us."

She looked up at him, her brown eyes wide and searching. "I thought you said no one is expecting us until supper?"

He turned away. She wasn't making this easy. "Well, after we take care of the horses and get cleaned up…"

Her smile died. "Oh." He didn't miss the disappointment in her voice. "Thanks, Linc, for bringing me up here today."

"You're welcome."

She started toward the horses and he reached for her arm to stop her. "Meg." He drew a long breath. "I don't want to take you back, but hell, I made you a promise yesterday and I'm trying my damnedest not to break it."

She looked confused. "Promise?"

"I told you I'd let you have a chance to think about us. I've been pushing you pretty hard. But I can't seem to make it through twenty-four hours without—" He pulled off his hat and raked a hand through his hair in frustration.

He watched her bite down on her lip. "Without what?" she asked innocently.

"Kissing you." His eyes never leaving hers, he moved closer. "I've wanted to kiss you since the minute you walked into the corral."

A soft blush set her cheeks aglow and she whispered, "So did I."

Linc's pulse began to race as he drew her into his arms. "Then I guess we've both been wasting a lot of time." He lowered his head and his mouth closed over hers.

Chapter Six

At 5:30 that evening Linc sat at the supper table. Even though Dora had prepared pot roast, he had no appetite. Nikki had been talking nonstop since she sat down, but he couldn't focus on what she had said. His only interest was in the woman seated across the table. Meg.

Suddenly she looked up at him and he had trouble breathing. He wasn't the only one affected. Meg blushed and her beautiful brown eyes darted back to Nikki. Was she thinking about this afternoon, their kiss? Maybe he should say kisses. What was supposed to be one kiss had turned into another, then another, leaving them both breathless. Finally Linc had pulled away, but seeing her swollen mouth nearly drove him back into her arms. Somehow he'd convinced them both to head home.

The ride back was silent, neither one of them wanting to make conversation. Linc had to fight with himself to keep from jerking Meg off her horse and onto his lap. And if he had, a few sweet, chaste kisses wouldn't be enough to satisfy him.

He heard his name called and shook his head to find Nikki staring at him. "What's wrong with you?"

He put down his fork. "Nothing, just tired. Remember, I've been up since five."

"You're up at five every day," Nikki countered. "Maybe you're just getting old and need to take a nap."

"Maybe you're such a smart mouth, you need a nap," Linc teased, and glanced at Meg to see her trying to hide a grin.

"You and who else is going to make me?"

Linc raised an eyebrow. "Sounds like a challenge to me." He slid his chair back and got up. Nikki's eyes widened as he grabbed her and his hands attacked her ribs.

"No," she cried, but soon broke into giggles when he began tickling her. "Okay! Okay, you're not old. Uncle."

He stopped and hugged Nikki to him, then kissed the top of her head. "Just remember that."

Nikki collapsed in her chair. "Aren't I getting a little too big for you to tickle?"

Linc glanced at Meg, then back at his sister. Nikki was right, she was growing up. Next year she would be in high school. "I guess so, but it's hard to get used to change."

"Try harder." She reached over and kissed her brother on the cheek. "I have a favor to ask you."

He folded his arms across his chest. "Oh no. Here it comes."

Nikki rolled her eyes. "I talked to Julie Newton today and she asked if I could spend the weekend. We want to go riding together. Do you think I can go?" The girl's dark eyes danced to Meg. "I promise to catch up on all my schoolwork, and clean my room, and—"

"Whoa, Nikki." Linc held up his hand. "First let me check this out with the Newtons."

His sister's smile faded. "You think I'm lying?"

Linc sat up straight. "No, honey. I think we have to check this out with all parties involved." He'd love nothing better than to see his sister friends again with a nice girl like Julie. "We'll check with your counselor."

"If Dr. Kathy says it's okay, can I go?" she asked.

Linc nodded. "You can go."

The girl jumped up and down, then hugged her brother before rushing out of the room. "I'm going to tell Julie."

"Nothing's definite," he called after her, but she was already gone.

Meg sat there watching Linc's satisfied grin. He loved Nikki and it showed. Meg was even a little envious of their relationship. Nikki was her sister, too, but Meg couldn't even let her know that she loved her. Would she ever be able to?

"You're awfully quiet," Linc said, breaking into her thoughts.

She looked at him. "I guess I'm a little tired."

He got up, came around the table and pulled her into his arms. "The ride wear you out?" he asked as he bent his head and began to nibble along her neck.

"A little." She gasped. "Linc! You shouldn't be doing this. Dora or Nikki could come..." Her words trailed off as his lips worked magic.

He raised his head. "Maybe we should do something about that." His dark eyes were searching hers. "I want to spend more time with you than just an occasional ride when we can fit it in."

"We do spend time together. I've been living here for well over a month."

"No, I'm always working out in the arena and you're busy in here. We see each other in passing and there are too many other distractions. And as much as I love my sister, she's a handful. And underfoot since she's been out of school. So I was thinking that if she goes to the Newtons for the weekend, what's to keep us from spending some time together?"

Meg tried not to panic but it wasn't easy. Being alone

with Linc was dangerous. She was halfway in love with the man as it was. "What did you have in mind?"

"I have to go to San Antonio to check out some horses. I've been putting it off." His gaze met hers. "I'd like to fly down this weekend, and I want you to go with me."

Meg pulled out of his arms and turned away. "I can't."

He came up behind her. "Why? Nikki will be gone. And you haven't taken a day off since you started working here." He paused. "Unless it's me you don't want to be with."

Meg swung around. Her mouth opened, but no words came out. Oh, yes, she wanted to be with him. It scared her how much she'd come to care for Linc. "It's not that."

"Look, Meg. I want you, you already know that. But I'm not going to pressure you into anything you're not ready for. Besides, if you agree to go with me to San Antonio, we'll have separate rooms."

Meg released a soft sigh and looked up at Linc's handsome face, feeling the heat from his intense gaze. One time couldn't hurt. "Maybe if Nikki's counselor says it's okay to leave her..."

He smiled. "So if the doc agrees, you'll go with me?"

Meg heard a warning bell in her head, but she knew it was already too late. "I'll go."

Early Saturday morning, Meg climbed out of the four-seater Cessna 182. The adrenaline was still racing through her body from her first ride in the small plane. Of course it had been her first time in any type of airplane. Linc had guessed that when he noticed her white-knuckle grip on the arms of her seat.

He had taken the time to coax her through her fears, telling her that he had been afraid the first time he went up. Then he placed his hand on hers and told her that he wouldn't let anything happen to her.

Meg had never felt so safe. All her life, she had been

the one who made sure that everyone had been taken care of. After her father died, she had been the one who kept food on the table and figured out a way to pay the bills. She'd never been able to depend on anyone. She'd glanced across the small plane at Linc. Would he be there for her? To protect her? To love her? Meg had almost gasped. Did she love Linc Stoner?

"Look out to your right." He'd pointed. "There's San Antonio."

Meg had glanced down at the busy city, excitement rushing through her as she pushed any worries out of her head. This was to be just a weekend away. She wasn't going to think of anything but having a good time, and spending it with Linc.

Once they'd landed, Linc had helped Meg out of the plane and taken their bags out and tossed them on the ground.

As soon as he secured the Cessna, he walked over to her.

"Well, how did you like your first look of Texas from the air?"

"I loved it." She smiled. "It was like a roller-coaster ride."

He looked hurt. "I hoped my flying skills were a little better than that."

"They were," she rushed to apologize. "I just meant that sometimes it was like we were floating and my stomach felt a little funny."

He leaned closer and whispered, "I was hoping my kisses had that effect on you."

"Oh, they do," she began before she realized what she admitted. "I mean—"

Linc broke into laughter and put his arm around her shoulders. "Don't ever play poker, darlin', those big brown eyes of yours will give you away every time." He picked up their bags and they walked toward the terminal.

Thirty minutes later Linc had rented a car and they were headed for downtown.

Linc glanced across the seat at Meg. She had been ignoring him since they got in the car. He didn't mind, though. She'd been busy looking out the window at her new surroundings. He'd discovered, before today, that Meg hadn't traveled much. In fact, the past thirteen years she hadn't been more than fifty miles away from her home in Oklahoma. It tickled him that he was going to be the one to show her San Antonio.

He turned the car onto College Street, then drove into the garage of the Spanish-colonial-style hotel, La Mansion Del Rio. Usually on business trips he stayed close by the airport, but this time he wanted Meg to enjoy the quiet, romantic town.

The valet opened Meg's door and helped her out of the car. She waited as Linc tipped the bellman, then he hurried toward her and took her hand.

"Well, how do you like it?"

"It's beautiful." She glanced up at the cream-colored structure.

"It can't hold a candle to you," he breathed against her ear, causing a shiver to rush down her spine. "Come on, let's get checked in," he suggested, and tugged on her arm.

Meg nodded and allowed him to lead her inside the lobby. The red-tiled floors were partially covered with colorful rugs. A sitting area was arranged with large comfortable furniture in a Southwestern motif.

Meg drew a long breath and released it. She had never been anywhere like this, she thought, glancing down at her simple pair of dark slacks and white blouse, and all of a sudden felt out of place. Linc had told her to dress casual. Her gaze shifted to him, standing at the front desk. He had on a starched white, Western-cut shirt that was tucked into a pair of new-looking Wrangler jeans. A shiny belt buckle showed off his narrow waist and a black felt Stetson adorned his head. He turned to her and smiled and her heart did a flip. Why did casual have to look so good on him? He motioned for her to come to the desk.

"Victor would like to know if you'd like a river view or a courtyard view?"

She looked at the young man behind the desk, then back to Linc. "Whatever you want."

Again he smiled. "I've got what I want," he whispered, then turned back to Victor. "A suite with a view of the river."

Minutes later, they were in the elevator and headed to the third floor. After the bellman unlocked the door, he carried the bags into the suite, then into the master bedroom, where he placed the bags next to the king-size bed. He came out and handed Linc the key in exchange for a tip, and with a thank-you he left.

Once the suite door closed, Linc went into the bedroom and retrieved his duffel bag and carried it across the sitting area and tossed it on the bed in the other bedroom.

"I didn't think I needed to explain our sleeping arrangements to the hotel staff," he said as he made his way to her, then he leaned down and kissed her sweetly on the lips.

"Thank you," she murmured. He was making it easy for her, but she couldn't help but wonder if she had been the first of his women to want separate bedrooms.

"My daddy taught me that giving your word is easy, it's keeping it that's the hard part." He stepped back and took her hand, pulling her toward the French doors leading to the balcony. Pushing open the doors, he allowed her to step outside. Meg nearly gasped at the beautiful scene.

The San Antonio River was directly below her, winding its way through the quaint city. A brick bridge arched across the narrow waterway. People strolled along the banks, stopping to visit the many shops and restaurants.

Meg felt Linc's arm come around her waist. "Well, how do you like it?"

She glanced over her shoulder, enjoying his closeness. "I've never seen anything like this."

He sighed and there was a touch of sadness in his voice. "My parents came here whenever they could get away from the ranch."

There was a long silence as they both watched the quiet activity below, then finally Linc spoke. "Come on, we better get moving. I have some horses to look at before I can think about having you all to myself tonight." He guided her back inside and toward her bedroom. "Put on something you don't mind getting a little dirty."

The Lazy S Horse Ranch was about thirty miles outside San Antonio. "Owned and operated by Beth and Dave Sanders for the past twenty years," Meg read the sign, as Linc drove the car through the gate.

"Dave and Beth were best friends with mom and dad," Linc began. "In fact, they were on their way down here for a visit when they had the accident." There was a catch in his voice. "I'm glad Dave and Beth were around afterward," he finished.

"It's nice to have friends around at times like that," she said, staring out at the rolling grassland. Off in the distance she saw horses grazing. "When my mother died, the neighbors were there to help with the chores. The women brought over food and even helped me make the arrangements."

"Yeah, at Mom and Dad's funeral people came from all over the state," Linc informed her. "Beth and Dave stayed a few days afterward and helped me get things in order."

He turned the car off the road to the circular drive leading to the brick two-story house. A small woman in her fifties rushed out the door to meet them. She was dressed in jeans and a Western shirt and her gray hair was cut short.

Her arms spread wide as she nearly ran into Linc's embrace. "Oh, I'm so glad to see you." She kissed his cheek. Tears sprang to her eyes.

Linc stepped back. "Hey, you promised you wouldn't do that." He touched the older woman's face.

She swatted at his hand. "Well, if you came to visit more often…" Beth's gaze suddenly went to Meg and a brighter smile appeared.

Linc did the introductions. "Beth, this is Meg Delaney. Meg, this is Beth Sanders."

Beth readily offered her hand. "So nice to meet you, Meg." The older woman gave her a curious stare. "You look familiar. Delaney… Delaney… Is your family from Mineral Wells?"

Meg started to panic. "No." She shook her head. "I'm from Oklahoma."

Linc came up behind her and placed his hands on her shoulders. "Meg's from a small town called Boswell. Her mother and Pauline were friends."

"What was your mother's name?"

Meg cleared her throat and managed to say, "Nina."

Beth looked confused. "I don't remember that name."

"It was a long time ago," Meg added, and was relieved when Linc began to talk.

"Meg's been doing a great job tutoring Nikki."

At the mention of Nikki, Beth's face lit up. "Where is that child anyway?"

"She's spending the weekend with her friend, Julie Newton," Linc said. "She's been working pretty hard this past month and I decided she needed some time off."

"And maybe you'd like some time alone yourself." The deep voice caused them all to turn around. A big, burly man stood with his hands on his narrow hips. He wore jeans and a Western shirt with a caramel-colored vest over it.

"Dave," Linc greeted him with a handshake, then a hug. The two men turned to the ladies. "I'd like you to meet Meg Delaney."

A slow smile crossed Dave Sanders's weathered face. He removed his hat, showing off his thinning gray hair. "Just like your daddy, you know how to pick out the pretty ones. Nice to meet you, Meg."

"Nice to meet you, too, Mr. Sanders."

Dave's smile broadened. "We go by first names around here, Meg."

Linc stood back and watched Meg as a soft blush spread over her face. He'd never known a woman who was so shy about receiving a simple compliment. He found it more and more appealing and wanted nothing more than to pull her into his arms and taste her sweet lips. Later, he told himself.

"Well, where are those new colts you've been braggin' about?"

"Just hold on," Dave chided. "We have all afternoon. Besides, I'd like to get to know this nice lady." He took Meg's hand and began to walk her toward the barn.

Frustrated, Linc watched Dave and Meg depart. He hadn't planned to spend the entire day at the ranch. He wanted time alone with Meg. The touch of Beth's hand caused him to look down at her.

"Dave's just teasin'," the older woman said assuredly. "We both know that you two young people don't want to spend the whole day with us. But I hope you'll at least stay for lunch."

He felt terrible. "It's not that—"

Beth raised her hand. "I know, son. I'm not so old that I can't remember what it's like to fall in love."

Linc froze. *In love?* No, he couldn't be.

Meg was more special to him than any woman in his

past, but they'd only known each other a few weeks. Then he recalled his dad telling him that he'd fallen in love with Pauline the first time he set eyes on her. Joe said there was no time limit to when you fall in love.

Linc heard his name called and his attention was drawn to Meg standing at the barn doors. She waved and his pulse suddenly rocketed. He watched her toss her long hair off her shoulders and adjust that silly straw cowboy hat she always wore.

"She is beautiful," Beth said. "All that blond hair and those big brown eyes. She's got a wholesome look that reminds me a lot of Nikki."

Linc wrinkled his forehead. "How can you think that? For one thing, their coloring is totally different."

"I know, but there's just something about her." Beth looked thoughtful. "How do the two get along?"

"Great. I owe Meg a lot. Nikki still is angry, but now, at least, we're talking about it. The counseling seems to be helping. And this weekend is the first time she wanted to spend time with her friend Julie."

They began walking toward the barn. "You mentioned on the phone that Nikki has been going to counseling."

"We both have." He was still embarrassed about having to go through such close scrutiny. "Not my favorite experience."

Beth smiled. "But it's helping your sister."

"Yeah. I just hope she appreciates it."

"I think both Nikki and Meg realize what a great guy you are."

Linc grinned. "If they don't, will you set 'em straight?"

Beth stopped and placed her hand on her hips. "You're darn right. And if you ever need anyone to help you with Nikki, you know that Dave and I are here."

"Thanks, Beth, I may take you up on that."

"I take it a thirteen-year-old is cramping your love life."

Linc felt his cheeks redden and Beth laughed as they walked through the barn doors. They found Meg and Dave at the end stall.

"Oh, Linc, you've got to see this guy," Meg said, kneeling down beside a two-week-old colt. The horse was the color of rich chocolate, with four white stockings and a blaze on his forehead.

"Meet Blazing Star," Dave announced.

Linc examined the animal. "Is this the one sired by Fire A Blaze?"

Dave nodded. "I bred Morning Star." He turned to Meg. "A few years back at an auction, I outbid Joe for Fire A Blaze."

"Looks like you got yourself one fine colt," Linc admitted.

"Old Joe always did have a good eye for horseflesh. He steered me in the right direction more than once. Come on, there's someone else I want you to meet." He led them out toward the corral. Dave gave a sharp whistle, and a long, leggy colt about six months old came running toward them. Linc couldn't help but stare at the beautiful chestnut horse as it skidded to a stop about ten feet away.

"I can usually catch him," Dave said. "But he might be a little shy with all the strangers."

Meg was the one who held out her hand and began speaking to the young animal. The colt bobbed its head up and down and neighed, but Meg continued her crooning as she reached out and grabbed hold of the halter.

"That's a good boy." She rubbed the colt's neck.

Linc and Dave approached the horse. "Linc, meet Starfire, a new stud for the Stoner Ranch."

Linc's gaze darted to Dave. "What are you talking about?"

The man took off his hat and scratched his head. "Your dad and I used to argue about how I tricked him out of

Blaze. The past few years, it left a bad feeling between us.''

"But, Dave, this guy, with his pedigree," Linc said as he examined the colt, "is a valuable animal."

"Not as valuable as my friendship was with your father. I had always planned on giving him the first foal anyway." Dave paused as emotions stopped his words. The older man glanced away, then back at Linc. "Starfire belongs on the Stoner Ranch."

Linc, too, was feeling a huge lump in his throat. "Thank you, Dave." He couldn't say any more as he walked over to his dad's friend and hugged him. Then they both turned to the horse.

Beth drew Meg away. "How about helping me with lunch and letting these two have some time?"

Once inside the big kitchen, Beth offered Meg some coffee. They sat down at the table to get to know each other.

"We offered to help Linc after the funeral, but he very nicely said, 'no thanks.' He wanted to care for Nikki. We hadn't exactly lost touch, but the boy wanted to handle things on his own. Even when the trouble with Nikki started, he didn't call us." Beth got up and refilled their cups with coffee. "I was a little hurt, but Dave explained that Linc was working through his own grief." She looked at Meg. "Do you know that Linc feels responsible for his parents' death?"

Meg nodded slowly. "For a while, Nikki blamed him, too. But thanks to counseling I think they're working through it."

"I'm glad. Joe and Pauline loved those kids so much. They'd hate it if their death was the cause of the problem."

"It seems that both Nikki and Linc can be stubborn," Meg admitted. "But they love each other." She looked up and realized that Beth had been staring at her.

The woman only smiled, then said, "Linc said that you and Nikki are getting along great."

Meg felt rising panic at the woman's close scrutiny, wondering if she had guessed her secret. "At first we didn't, but we do pretty well now."

"Are you planning on staying in the area after she goes back to school?"

Meg wasn't deceiving herself. She knew her tutoring job was close to ending. She had to think about leaving the ranch and getting on with her life. "I'm not sure what I'm going to do. I have a friend in Fort Worth and she's invited me to stay with her."

Beth raised an eyebrow. "What about Linc?"

Meg avoided her eyes. "Linc knows I'll be leaving."

The older woman got up from the table and walked to the back door, opening it for the men coming up on the porch. "That doesn't mean he's going to like it."

What Beth had said stayed with Meg all afternoon, and later that evening when Linc took her out to dinner at a seafood restaurant near the hotel. The food was delicious, but Meg had barely tasted it. What if Beth discovered who she was? Worse, what if she told Linc?

"You ready to go?"

"What?" Meg jumped, then realized it was Linc. "Sure."

He helped her with her chair and escorted her out of the restaurant. He took her hand as they strolled along the river walk.

"You've been awful quiet tonight."

"So much has happened. And we were up pretty early."

His arm closed around her shoulder and pulled her against him. "And here I thought it was my company."

"Oh, no," she said quickly. "You've shown me such a wonderful time. I can't begin to thank you."

He tossed her a sexy smile. "I'll think of a way."

Meg's heart skipped a beat. She'd just bet he could.

"Come on, let's go back to the hotel." He nudged her along as they walked through the crowd, and a short time later they entered the hotel lobby.

The ride up the elevator was silent, but his look to her was one of passion. It frightened and intrigued her, leaving her wanting for something she'd never had. She didn't have any illusions about a future with Linc. With her secret, there never could be any between them. But, if just for a little while, she wanted to stop the ache, she wanted him to love her.

The bell chimed and they got off on the fourth floor. He held her close to his side as they walked down the hall. Meg felt the erotic friction of her red dress moving against his jeans-covered thigh. They stopped at their room and Linc pulled out the key, but before he opened the door he bent his head and kissed her.

Meg gasped at the pure pleasure. Linc, too, was affected as he drew her against his body, deepening the kiss. Suddenly there were voices and Linc raised his head.

"We need more privacy." He opened the door and took her inside. No sooner had the door closed than his mouth was back on hers. Her hands touched his chest, moving upward and circling his neck. Meg no longer listened to her common sense as she, too, gave in to the hunger. Whatever strength she had was gone. She wanted Linc, and he wanted her.

Linc felt as if he'd wanted Meg for an eternity. His hands held her face as his tongue shot into her mouth, trailing over her lips and teeth, taking everything she offered.

His hands worked between them, and he heard her sharp breath as he tugged at the buttons on her dress. He parted the fabric and unfastened the clasp on her bra. This time he was the one who groaned as he cupped her full breasts, testing the weight in his hands, then his thumbs gently caressed the nipples to taut peaks.

She cried out and collapsed against him. Linc picked her up in his arms and carried her into her bedroom. The moonlight from the window flooded against the bed in a soft glow. He set Meg on the floor and pulled the comforter off, then returned to her arms.

"Oh, Meg, I want you." His mouth took hers again.

"I want you too," she confessed softly, nearly bringing him to his knees.

He tugged her dress off her shoulders and pulled it down to her waist, then helped her step out of it, and she kicked off her shoes. She stood before him, naked except for her white high-cut panties.

"Damn, but you're pretty," he breathed as he unbuttoned his shirt and quickly stripped it off.

Next came his belt, then he pulled open the metal snap on his jeans as he kissed her long and hard. His hands traced the swell of her hips, his fingers finding every curve. About ready to explode, he broke off the kiss and laid her down on the bed. He sat on the edge of the mattress, jerked off his boots and tossed his jeans aside, then joined her.

His breathing was rapid as he stretched out next to her and took her mouth in a searing kiss. Then he moved partially on top of her and suddenly she stiffened.

He pulled back. "Meg, what's wrong?"

She shook her head, but refused to look at him.

"Meg, if you're not ready for this…" He was going to die if she'd changed her mind.

"It's not that I don't want you. It just that…that I've never been with…anyone." She looked up at him, her eyes large and searching.

Oh, no! Her confession stopped him cold, leaving him frustrated, but also thrilled at the thought she wanted him as she had no other man. With his last ounce of willpower he rolled to the edge of the mattress and sat up.

"Linc, I'm sorry."

"No, Meg. I'm sorry. I promised you that I wouldn't rush you tonight and here I am all over you." He felt her hand on his back and he trembled. He had to get the hell out of here. He stood and picked up his clothes and boots. "I'll see you in the morning."

"Linc," Meg called to him. He turned around and saw her sitting up, holding the sheet against her naked body, her hair all gold and wild. Damn!

"Look, Meg. Right now isn't a good time to talk. I'll see you in the morning." He walked out, closed the door and leaned against it. Damn. This had to be love. Otherwise, dynamite wouldn't have driven him out of her bed.

Chapter Seven

The following weekend, Linc walked into the den and shut the door, cutting off the loud music coming from the second floor. It sounded like a rock concert instead of a sleepover for Nikki and five of her friends.

Linc sank into the leather chair behind the oak desk with a sigh. Ah, silence. He glanced around the knotty-pine-paneled room. The floor-to-ceiling bookcase covering the wall dulled the noise considerably.

"Not exactly soundproof, but it'll do," he said, thinking he might just sleep here tonight, eyeing the long sofa by the fireplace. His thoughts turned to Meg. How was she handling all the commotion? The last he'd seen of her was when he walked past Nikki's bedroom. Meg was right in the middle of the crazy activity, doing whatever it was that girls did when they got together.

He leaned back in the chair wishing Meg wanted to be with him instead of in a room full of noisy thirteen-year-olds? Why couldn't she join him, steal a little time for the two of them?

But that wasn't going to happen tonight.

Things between them had cooled since he'd walked out of her room that night in San Antonio. It was his own fault. He hadn't been able to face his own feelings, let alone deal with Meg's. He closed his eyes as the scene in the hotel room flashed through his head. Meg naked and willing in bed.

Every lonely night of the past week, his aching body had reminded him how much he'd wanted her. Still wanted her. He shot out of the chair and started to pace. God, he'd never wanted a woman so much. But you didn't take a woman like Meg to bed and just get up and leave the next morning. She was the kind of woman who expected... He stopped pacing. Expected what? Love? Marriage?

What did he expect? He closed his eyes, remembering her touch, the feel of her mouth against his, her beautiful eyes, the soft blush on her cheeks, the way she smiled when she sat on a horse. The thrill he got when she turned that smile on him. Linc knew that Meg would never have wanted to make love to him if she hadn't cared for him deeply. And what had he done? He had gotten up and walked out on her when she had been the most vulnerable.

Worst of all, they hadn't talked since that night a week ago. They flew back to the ranch in silence, and he'd been avoiding her ever since. It was time he explained things. Make Meg understand it was for the best, that he didn't have the luxury of thinking about a personal life until things were straightened out with Nikki.

He turned to the mounds of paperwork piled on the table behind the desk. For months the family lawyer had been asking him to go through his dad's papers. This was a good time to sort through the mess. The faint sound of music rumbled through the room. What else did he have to do?

Linc went to the cabinet and opened the door, exposing a wall safe. He worked the familiar combination, then pulled open the door. Drawing a breath, he reached inside for the accordion file folder that contained stock certificates, bonds, insurance policies and birth certificates. Linc returned to the desk, untied the cord and began sorting through the contents. He found several different insurance policies, along with his parents' marriage license. There was a tightening in his chest when he realized that this fall they would have been married thirty-five years.

Next he pulled out his birth certificate and his adoption papers, then set them aside and reached for Nikki's. He smiled when he opened the papers and read what was written. Nicole Pauline Stoner, born in Mineral Wells, Texas, on September 13, at 2:08 a.m.

"And you're still a night owl," he murmured, listening to the noise from upstairs. She had weighed six pounds, two ounces, and been eighteen inches long. Linc could still remember how tiny she had seemed when Pauline and Joe brought her home. His gaze dropped down on the page, searching for the name of her biological parents. He frowned. He didn't know they gave that out.

Suddenly air was trapped in his lungs as he read the names.

Mother: Nina Morgan Delaney. Father: Ralph Gene Delaney.

"My God!" His pounding pulse was deafening in his ears. "Meg is Nikki's sister?" His voice echoed in the empty room as he collapsed into the chair. Pain and anger tore at his gut as he studied the document once again, hoping he'd read it wrong. But there wasn't any mistake. The name Delaney stood out on the page as if it were a neon sign.

"Damn! She lied to me," he hissed. He tossed the paper on the desk and tore out of the room. Taking the stairs two steps at a time, he tried to calm himself. Once at Nikki's bedroom door, he knocked and heard the girls inside quiet down.

Nikki answered and Linc's gaze quickly scanned her

features. Why hadn't he seen the resemblance? The shape of her face, her eyes.

"Linc, you promised you wouldn't bother us." The thir- teen-year-old was overdone with makeup and her hair was piled on top of her head.

He raised his palm. "I'm not, but I need to see Meg." He had trouble getting her name out. "Please have her come down to the den as soon as possible."

Nikki nodded. "Okay."

Linc returned to the office. He paced impatiently for a few minutes, then there was a knock on the door and Meg walked in.

She stood in the doorway feeling ridiculous. The girls had made her face up and her hair was teased. But Linc had asked to see her and she hadn't wanted to take the time to change. Now seeing how handsome and serious he looked, she wished she had.

She swallowed. "You wanted to see me?"

He placed his hands on his hips. "Close the door."

Meg did as he asked and moved toward the desk. "Is there something wrong?"

"How long did you think you could get away with it?"

Meg's heart stopped. She glanced down at the paper on the desk. It looked like some sort of official document, a birth certificate. Oh, God, it was Nikki's birth certificate. He knew. Trembling, she met his accusing stare. No matter what she said, she knew he wasn't going to believe her.

"Did you hear me?"

"Yes," she answered, finding the courage to speak. "But I think you've already made up your mind about things."

He drew a slow breath and folded his arms across his chest. "Try me."

Meg eyed the door with foolish thoughts of escaping. But it was too late. She clutched her hands together to stop the shaking and squared her shoulders. "I didn't know Nikki existed until my mother died."

He cocked an eyebrow.

"It's true," she insisted. "I was told that the baby my mother was pregnant with back then had died at birth."

Again no response, only his cold stare. This couldn't be the same man she'd nearly made love to a week ago.

"It wasn't until the last stages of my mother's cancer that she talked about the baby she'd lost, the baby she'd given away. At first I thought it was the effects of the medication, but there was something in her voice that made me listen...wonder if what she was saying could possibly be true."

Meg walked to the fireplace. She needed more space. "Just before my mother died, she begged me to find her baby, to see if she was all right. I promised I would." Tears pooled in her eyes, but she refused to let them fall. "When she told me the Stoners were the family who adopted my sister, I was shocked. I'd only been eleven, but I remembered driving by your ranch back when Dad worked at the Logan place up the road."

"I don't recall any trainer around here by the name of Delaney," Linc said.

Meg lowered her eyes. No way was she going to humiliate herself by telling Linc that her father had lost most of his jobs because of his drinking. "We weren't in the area long," she murmured.

Linc combed his hand through his hair, looking as if he were fighting his own demons. "Just long enough to have a child and give it up. Why, Meg?"

This time she glanced away. "From what my mother told me, we didn't have a whole lot. Jobs were scarce and Dad couldn't find work. With three kids already, they couldn't afford another baby. Dad had heard the Stoners wanted a child."

"So you're saying our parents got together and arranged an adoption?"

Meg nodded. Thanks to her father, she thought bitterly. She still wasn't sure it had been totally legal. "And I promised my mother that I'd find out if she were happy."

"And after you saw the way your sister lived, you decided to hang around."

Meg's hands clenched into fists. There was no reasoning with this man. "I didn't come here to purposely deceive anyone, Linc. When I arrived at the ranch, I was planning on telling your parents who I was. I had no idea about the accident that took their lives. Besides, it was you who jerked me through the door and practically begged me to stay. What would you have done in my place?"

"Tell the truth."

She gave him a doubting look. "Sure you would. You'd walk into a situation with a social worker involved, find out your sister has been ditching school and running away, and the first words out of the thirteen-year-old's mouth are 'I hate you.'" Meg took a needed breath. "Wouldn't you stick around and try to help?"

"Especially when you discovered she would be half-owner of a very successful horse ranch," Linc answered.

It felt as if his words had pierced her heart. He just didn't understand. "I stayed because you both needed me. Nikki would be in a foster home if it weren't for me."

"You're so generous," he added, his eyes stony with anger. "What else were you willing to do to help your sister?"

She gasped, and before she could stop herself, reached out and slapped him. Her breath caught as she watched the red mark slashed across his cheek. "Oh, God!" She turned and hurried to the door, but before she could get it open, Linc grabbed her arm.

"Let me go," she cried, trying to break away. It was no use. He drew her against him.

Linc felt lower than a snake. "Shh, Meg," he said as he continued to hold her. Since he'd found a home at the ranch, he promised himself he'd never intentionally set out to hurt another person the way his dad had. But this woman, who'd already stolen his heart, was capable of destroying the only family he had left.

"I'll never let you take Nikki," he whispered into her hair.

She shook her head and pulled back. "That was never my intention. It was the truth when I said I was on my way to Fort Worth for a job interview. I only stopped by to tell the Stoners who I was and to ask that maybe someday, when Nikki turned eighteen, I could meet her."

Linc wanted to believe her. He ran his hand through his hair. His gaze went back to Meg. Her big brown eyes were smeared with mascara, her soft blond hair curled and wild around her face. She was so beautiful, and his body was telling him that he wanted her as much as ever. But things were different now. She had the power to take Nikki from him. Given the blood ties and his poor history of raising his sister, the courts might give Meg custody. He couldn't let that happen.

Linc reached into his pocket for his handkerchief and handed it to her. "You sure as hell can't tell Nikki who you are."

He watched Meg's eyes widen, then turn sad. "I know. I'll pack my clothes and be gone in the morning." She handed back the handkerchief and started for the door.

Linc balled his hands into fists to keep from reaching out for her, begging her to stay. But all he could do was watch her walk out of the room and out of his life. It was all for the best, he thought, feeling the knot tighten in his stomach.

He had to protect what was left of his family.

For the first time since she had arrived at the ranch, Meg wasn't at the table when Linc came downstairs for breakfast. Dora gave him a puzzled look, but he just ignored her and sat down. He wasn't in the mood for a lot of questions this morning. He'd done what he had to do, and that was that.

"Where's Meg?"

"How would I know?" he answered, then took a swallow of coffee.

The housekeeper set a plate of eggs and bacon in front of him, then jammed her hand on her hips. "You haven't been able to keep your eyes off her since the moment she set foot on the ranch and suddenly you don't know where she is?"

His lack of privacy in his own home irritated him. "That's right," he grumbled.

"I know you two have been avoiding each other lately," she continued, "since your trip to San Antonio."

"Leave it alone, Dora," he warned.

"You ever think she could be sick or something?"

Linc picked up his fork. "She isn't sick. She's packing."

The housekeeper looked confused. "Packing?"

Linc didn't feel so hot himself. Meg had hurt him with her lies. And the last thing he wanted was more questions. "She's decided to leave."

"I can't hardly believe that. She seems so happy here." Dora's voice faded, then quickly she got a determined look. "And you're just going to let her walk out of here? Meg Delaney is the best thing that has happened to this family, and Nikki adores her, and you're not gonna do a thing to stop her."

Linc opened his mouth to defend himself, when Nikki came rushing into the room. "Is it true?" The girl's face was flushed. "Is Meg leaving?"

He put his fork down. Hell, he wasn't hungry anyway. "Yes, she is."

"Why?" Her voice became bitter. "Did you do something to make her leave?"

"No. I didn't do anything." He had to turn away from her accusing stare. "It's just better this way."

"For you maybe. But not for me." Nikki pleaded, "I don't want Meg to go. Please, Linc."

He stood and reached for his sister. He wanted to erase the pain in her face. "I'm here, Nikki. We don't need anyone else."

The thirteen-year-old jerked away. "No, it's not the same," she said pleadingly. "I need Meg, too. She understands." Then her words turned venomous. "Why do you take everyone I love away? First Mom and Dad. Now Meg."

Linc felt as if she'd stuck a knife in his gut. She did blame him. "That's not true, Nik. I'm here and I love you."

"No, you don't." She swiped at her tears. "If you did you wouldn't let Meg go away. I hate you," she yelled as she rushed out of the kitchen. A few seconds later the sound of her bedroom door slamming seemed to rock the house.

Linc sat there in stunned silence. His anger turned into an empty ache—the same one he'd had since he found out about Joe and Pauline's accident. Dammit! Now he was losing Nikki and there wasn't anything he could do about it. He shoved his chair away from the table and grabbed his hat off the peg on the wall and jammed it on his head. He had to get out of there. "I'll be back around supper," he called to Dora as he pushed open the back door.

"Just hold right there, Lincoln Stoner," Dora ordered.

Linc stopped on the edge of the porch but didn't turn around. She hadn't used that tone with him since he was a kid.

"You're as bad as your sister! That's your solution?

You're just gonna run away, too, and not do a dang thing about that child upstairs?''

Dammit, didn't she know he had tried—tried for the past six months—but nothing had worked with Nikki. He hadn't felt so helpless in years, not since his father had come home drunk and used him as a punching bag. Linc turned and stared at the housekeeper through the screen door. ''Nikki's not about to listen to anything I have to say. She needs time to cool off.''

''She needs a firm hand, and to know that someone loves her.''

Well, right now that someone wasn't him, Linc thought as he pushed his hat back off his forehead. Didn't Dora realize that?

''You're taking away the only person since your parents death who's has been able to reach Nikki. Your only hope is getting Meg to stay.''

''I can't,'' Linc growled. She had lied to him. At the beginning he could have understood it, but after they'd gotten so close…

''I thought you two had something special goin'.''

He'd thought they had, too. That was the part that hurt so much. ''That's over.''

Dora looked doubtful. ''Are you sure? From where I stood it looked like a lot of sparks were flyin' between the two of you.''

''Dammit, Dora,'' Linc growled.

''Don't you cuss at me, Linc Stoner. You've been moonin' over that sweet gal since she got here. If you had any sense, you'd grab her and get a preacher out here and put yourself out of your misery.'' She folded her arms across her ample chest and smiled as if her suggestion wasn't the least bit outrageous. ''And I doubt if Meg would be contrary to the idea either,'' she offered. ''Then you could both concentrate on making a stable home for that poor girl upstairs.''

"That's the craziest idea I've ever heard," Linc said, but his mind was reeling. Dora might have just come up with the most concrete solution to his problem.

But marriage. Hell and damnation!

He walked to the porch railing and looked out at the rich green pastures he'd loved from the moment he set foot on the Stoner Ranch. But it hadn't been the ranch that had made him feel secure, it had been the love Joe and Pauline had lavished on him. And right now he needed to get through to Nikki that he loved her, too, and would always be there for her.

But if he didn't think of something fast, the breach between him and Nikki could widen, could become permanent. Meg might take him to court and sue for custody. And she'd have a hell of a good chance of getting it, especially since Nikki and she were blood relatives. If Nikki were asked to choose, it was pretty clear who she'd pick.

Panic surged through him and he slapped his hand against the railing. He'd be damned if he'd lose his sister. He'd do whatever it took to keep them together. Even if that meant marrying his competition.

Determined, he bolted into the house and pulled open the screen. Dora quickly stepped aside as he went through the kitchen. In the dining room he picked up his pace and headed for the stairs. When he arrived at Meg's room, before he changed his mind, he raised his hand and knocked firmly.

After a few seconds the door swung open and Meg appeared before him. She was dressed in a pair of dark slacks and a white ribbed top. Her hair was pulled back in curls and he ached to run his hands through the soft strands…and so much more.

"If you came to see if I'm packed, I am." She pointed over her shoulder. "I left Nikki's lesson plans on the dresser for the next tutor." She sighed. "If you'll just help me carry my things downstairs—"

"The hell I will." He stepped into her room. "You're not going anywhere."

Her eyes widened. "You want me to stay?"

He couldn't bring himself to admit anything to her. "Do I have a choice?"

"I don't understand. I thought you wanted me to leave."

"I'm thinking of Nikki now. If you leave, she'll be the one who suffers. She wants you here. I know my sister, Meg, she's stubborn as a mule." He combed his hand through his hair. "If you don't stay, she may run away again. And I'll lose her for sure."

Meg tried to stay calm, but she couldn't control the surge of joy that shot through her. Even if it was only for Nikki, Linc wanted her to stay. "You know she's been asking about her birth parents. What are you going to do?"

"When she's older I'll tell her."

"She'll be angry with you for keeping it a secret."

"Look, Nikki's had a lot to deal with lately. She doesn't need another complication."

Meg didn't agree with Linc's thinking. Keeping this big secret would be difficult. Maybe impossible. And if Nikki found out by accident, she'd be furious.

But another problem was Meg's feelings for Linc. Could she stay here loving him and knowing how much he resented her? Linc Stoner had the upper hand, all right. He was Nikki's legal guardian, and if Meg didn't go along with his plan, he could keep her from ever seeing her sister again.

She looked up at him. "All right, Linc. I'll stay until I finish the tutoring job. Once Nikki is in summer school—"

"No!" he blurted out. "You have to stay indefinitely." His voice softened. "Nikki needs both of us."

Her heart raced again with a fleeting hope. "What are you trying to say?"

Linc wasn't sure of anything anymore. He only knew that he couldn't lose Nikki. He would do anything to keep that from happening, and there was only one way he could think to prevent it. "We have to get married," he blurted out.

Meg froze, unable to breathe. "Married?" she gasped. "Are you out of your mind?"

He raised a calming hand. "I know the idea sounds crazy, but think about it. It would solve the problem without telling Nikki who you are, and you could be around to keep an eye on me and make sure I'm doing a good job of parenting."

"Hold it," Meg interrupted, her hopes dashed. "Do I understand that you want to marry me to help you raise Nikki?"

Linc nodded, obviously confident that all he had to do was present Meg with the plan and she'd agree. "Call it a business arrangement until Nikki reaches eighteen."

Meg was trying hard to stay calm. All she could think about was how her father had controlled her mother all of her life. Nina Delaney had even given up a child to please the man. Well, the same thing wasn't going to happen to Meg. No matter how much she loved Linc, she wouldn't allow him to arrange her life just to suit himself and his plans. Did he think he could bend her to his will just like he did the thoroughbreds in the arena?

"Meg…"

She looked at him. His handsome face was determined, sure. "Your idea is crazy, Linc."

"Why? We've gotten along pretty well so far. We both care about Nikki and want her to be happy. She'll be of age in five years. It isn't so long. You could go to school and get your degree. As my wife, you would get a generous allowance and wouldn't have to work, other than supervising Nikki." He raised an eyebrow. "You planned to go to college when you moved to Fort Worth, didn't you?"

Meg could only nod as she looked up at his dark, mesmerizing eyes. Her stomach did a somersault. Damn the man! He made it sound so reasonable.

"Well, Meg?" He stepped closer and reached for her hand, tugging her toward him until their bodies were nearly touching and she felt his heat.

"Stay," he breathed as his head descended toward hers. "Marry me." When his mouth touched hers, she sighed softly, but quickly came to her senses and jumped back. She couldn't let this happen.

"No! That's not going to get you what you want. Nikki has to be our first concern." She glared at him. "Have you asked her what she thinks about this so-called marriage?"

He shrugged. "Since she isn't talking to me, how could I?"

"Where is she?"

"She's in her room." He looked at Meg. "Maybe you should go after her and tell her you're going to stay and marry me."

Meg froze. What was she going to do? She was in love with this man, but how did he feel about her? Was she willing to take him on any terms, a man who didn't trust her, just for Nikki's sake? "You're assuming a lot since I haven't agreed to anything. And since I have no idea what you are offering me, a real marriage, or a business proposition."

He sobered. "Maybe that's a bad way to put it. Let's just say we'll both have a part in raising Nikki. As for the rest…" With a shrug, he came closer, and Meg knew he wasn't talking about Nikki now. "I won't force you into anything, Meg." His voice was husky, causing a warm shiver to rush down her spine.

"Uh, are you sure we can't sit Nikki down and explain about her adoption?" Meg stammered, suddenly anxious to change the subject.

He shook his head. "Not yet."

Meg wanted to argue, but his stubborn look told her it would be useless. "So, if I say yes, my only duties as your wife will be to oversee the house and supervise Nikki?"

Linc nodded slowly. He clenched his hands together, trying not to show his nervousness. He found he wanted Meg to say yes to his proposal, instead of to his business arrangement. The anger he'd been feeling the past twelve hours seemed to be diminishing. Now all he could think about was doing whatever he could to keep Meg Delaney in his life.

"When Nikki goes to school, so can you. I promise I'll do my part to help share responsibilities. I'm not just going to leave you to do it all by yourself. Nikki needs both of us." And I need you, too, Meg, he thought silently.

Meg stared at Linc for a long moment. "I'll stay as Nikki's tutor until summer school starts, but the other part I have to think about." She folded her arms across her chest. "Is that acceptable?"

"I guess it will have to be. But don't wait too long."

"Give me until next week," she said.

"You got it."

"Okay, I'll go see how Nikki is." She stepped around Linc and headed off to find her sister, certain that this was the craziest situation she'd ever been in.

During the next week, Meg had a rough time. Between trying to tutor Nikki and mulling over Linc's proposition, she hadn't slept well at all. She still hadn't come to any conclusion and she was running out of time. Maybe a swim would help relax her, she thought as she stepped through the French doors onto the patio. The evening was warm and sultry for early June, but that wasn't what really drew her to the pool. No, that wasn't the reason. She had been watching Linc from her bedroom window, seeing him dive into the cool water. That's what had brought her downstairs. She had been avoiding him all week. Now, as she stood in the doorway watching his imposing body glistening as he climbed out of the pool, she nearly panicked but forced herself to stay.

Linc reached for a towel draped over the chair and began wiping the water from his face and hair. Meg's eyes were glued to his broad chest, remembering the feel of his skin. She licked her lips as her gaze combed over his flat stomach and long, muscular legs. She drew a deep breath but that didn't help steady her heart rate.

Suddenly he looked up and caught her staring. "So you finally decided to stop avoiding me."

"I told you I needed time," she said bravely. "After all, it wasn't exactly a standard marriage proposal."

Linc wrapped the towel around his neck. "If you want hearts and flowers—"

"No!" She waved her hand in the air, but not before he saw what looked like hurt in her eyes. Damn! He was messing this up.

"As you said before, we have to think about Nikki," Meg finished.

"So, are you ready to give me an answer?" Lord. Why did he have to sound like such a jerk, he asked himself. He wouldn't blame her if she turned him down cold. If he wasn't careful he could lose both Nikki and Meg.

"Yes. I thought it over, and you're right, the best thing for Nikki right now is that the two of us try to give her a stable home."

He released the air from his lungs in relief. She was going to marry him. "So you agree?"

She ignored his question. "I still think that you should reconsider telling her the truth about me."

Panic surged through him again and he stepped closer. "I won't give in on that, Meg."

"Would you at least think about telling her, say in another year?"

"If and when the time is right," he answered.

He watched the emotions play across her face. "Nikki and I are building a pretty good relationship as friends," she said. Her big brown eyes met his. "I wouldn't want to mess that up. Maybe waiting a while wouldn't hurt."

"Then you'll marry me?"

Meg nodded. "Of course, as you said, it's not really a marriage as much as a business relationship."

Linc frowned. "I've been thinking about that. Do you really believe we're going to be able to keep this relationship platonic?" When he reached for her hand, he was thrilled that she didn't pull away. "I know we have strong feelings for each other. San Antonio proved that." He kissed the back of her hand and heard her suck in a breath. "I'd like to at least try, for Nikki's sake, to make a go of this marriage."

To prove the fact, he drew her against him and captured her lips in a heated kiss. His tongue pushed into her mouth, stroking deeply, demanding a response that Meg couldn't refuse.

"You see?" he said when they finally pulled apart. "I have no intention of being celibate for the next five years, or of going to other women." Linc moved against her, making her feel his desire. "Make no mistake, Meg Delaney, I want you every way a man wants his wife." His husky voice caused her to shiver even in the heated air. "Do you have a problem with that?"

Meg felt dazed. If only she could resist him. If only she didn't love him so. "No," she whispered.

"Good." He kissed her hard and long and Meg's knees threatened to give way.

"Does this mean that Meg is going to stay past summer school?"

They jumped apart just in time to discover Nikki standing outside the French doors.

Meg glanced up at Linc, her heart drumming in her chest.

"Don't you know it isn't nice to eavesdrop?" he growled.

The teenager stepped closer and smiled. "I called out, but I guess you were too busy to hear."

"Meg and I were discussing some things."

"Interesting way of putting it," Nikki said.

Linc tugged Meg against his side. "Well, how about this way of putting it—Meg has agreed to marry me."

The thirteen-year-old's gaze danced anxiously between Meg and her brother, then a grin spread across her face. "Really?"

Meg nodded. "Is that okay with you?" They'd never considered the fact that Nikki might not like the idea.

The girl jumped up and down, then nearly flung herself into the couple's arms. "I think it's great." She hugged them both. "I'm going to have a sister."

Meg shot a quick glance at Linc. He avoided her eyes.

"Actually, you're going to have a sister-in-law," Linc corrected.

"Who cares," Nikki said. "Meg's not going away. And she's going to be part of the family." Meg was hugged again. "Oh, wow! Are you two going to have a baby soon? I hope so. That means I'll be an aunt."

"Slow down, Nik," Linc protested. "Meg and I only decided to get married tonight. We haven't finalized all the details yet."

"Oh! I've got to call Julie," Nikki interrupted. She started for the house, then looked back at her brother. "This is the best thing that's happened in a long time."

"I'm glad you're happy. I just want us to be a family again."

Meg was touched by Linc's love for his sister. She found she was a little envious, too. If Linc could only care for her half as much, she'd be thrilled.

"Meg," Nikki begged. "Can I help you plan the wedding?"

Meg was at a loss. She hadn't thought about the ceremony, about when or where. "I don't need anything fancy."

"Of course you can help," Linc promised. "Now you go call your friend while I persuade my bride-to-be into having the wedding soon." He bent his head and kissed Meg while Nikki giggled on her way out.

Meg was a little breathless when Linc finally released her. "Now, I better leave or I'll forget my good intentions to keep my hands off you." His eyes locked with hers. "I'll try my damnedest to keep my distance until next week."

"Next week?"

"Yeah. I thought we could have the ceremony a week from Saturday," He waved a hand. "This should be as good a place as any."

"But it's so soon." She was panicking. "My brothers…"

"Do they know about Nikki?"

She shook her head. "No. My mother only told me."

"Then invite them." He frowned. "Unless you think they'll realize what's going on."

"They may wonder why we're rushing this."

"Just tell them the truth. We can't wait."

That brought a warm blush to Meg's cheeks, but she didn't look away.

"Damn, Meg. That look of yours turns me inside out." His hand came up and he stroked the side of her face. His expression softened. "But that doesn't mean I'm coming after you like a rutting stallion. I'll promise to do my best to make you happy. To please you." He moved back. "Good night, Meg." He turned and walked off, leaving her to collapse into a nearby chair.

"Oh, God, what have I gotten myself into?" she whispered into the night.

Chapter Eight

Linc paced the living room, occasionally stopping to glance out the double doors as the guests took their seats on the patio. The small wedding they'd planned had turned into a gathering of about fifty friends and neighbors. A florist, a bakery and a caterer had gotten involved when Nikki decided she was going to help with the wedding. And, as usual, Linc had let his sister have her way.

He checked his watch again. It was nearly two o'clock. Wasn't the ceremony supposed to start by two? he wondered, looking around for Meg. Nikki and Beth Sanders had kept her hidden from him all morning. Some damn superstition about it being unlucky for the groom to see the bride before the wedding. To his surprise, Linc discovered he'd missed Meg at breakfast. It was usually a time they shared together, just quiet conversation before their day began. He couldn't help but hope that after today they'd spend future early mornings…in bed. His body suddenly came to life, leaving no doubt how much he wanted Meg. But did she feel the same? Would she be willing to be with him tonight…and every night?

"Nervous?"

Linc turned around to find Dave Sanders. He was dressed in a tux, looking pleased and ready to perform his duties as best man. "Maybe a little," Linc said.

Dave patted him on the back. "It's natural, son. Just keep thinking about the wonderful gal that's gonna be sharing your life. You and Meg are both lucky to have found each other."

"Yeah," Linc agreed. They weren't exactly starting their marriage in the conventional way. But they could make it work. They had to, or he just might lose Nikki.

Suddenly the French doors opened and the minister came in and announced that he was ready to begin the ceremony. Linc took a deep breath and followed Dave to the front of the patio.

Upstairs, Meg stared at herself in the mirror. Her antique satin wedding dress was beautiful. She fingered the delicate lace along the low-cut neckline and the cap sleeves. She turned and admired the sculptured train that hung from her fitted waistline, trailing long past her hemline.

For years Nina Delaney had talked about her daughter's wedding, but Meg doubted her mother's dreams had included the elegant dress that Beth and Nikki helped her pick out. The price had been outrageous, but Linc had forbidden her to worry about the cost. But that was impossible. Money problems had been part of her growing up. The Delaneys never had anything but the scrap of acreage they'd managed to scrounge a living off of. That was Meg's past. The woman in the mirror, the one in this gorgeous dress, didn't look like she had any money problems. Meg swallowed back a sob. Not having money problems was part of the bargain she'd made with Linc. Suddenly she was feeling like a convenient bride.

Nikki came up behind her. "You look so beautiful."

Meg turned around and forced herself to smile. "You really think so?"

Nikki nodded and reached up to arrange the elbow-length veil. "Yes. Linc's gonna go crazy when he sees you."

A girl can always hope, Meg thought as she eyed her sister, dressed in a tea-length rose taffeta dress. "Talk about being a knockout. You look pretty good yourself."

The teenager glanced in the mirror. "I don't know."

"Oh, Nikki. You're growing into a beautiful woman." Meg hugged her.

"Well, I know I'm growing." She frowned. "I'm taller than most of the boys in my class."

Meg brushed the girl's dark curls away from her face. "I was, too, at your age. But that will change. It just takes a little longer for the boys to get their full height."

"If I turn out like you it'll be worth the wait."

"Why, thank you." Had it been only a few months ago that this girl couldn't say a kind word to anyone? "I'm happy you agreed to be my maid of honor. I want so much for us to be a family."

Tears filled Nikki's eyes. "So do I. And I'm glad you're marrying my brother. Now I'll have the sister I always wanted."

Meg bit her lower lip to hold back the tears. This was what she'd always wanted, too. But she had to keep it a secret. Her thoughts turned to her mother's dying wish. At least Meg was keeping her promise. She was making sure that Nikki was being taken care of. "That means a lot to me, Nikki. I'll try my best to be the one you hoped for."

There was a knock on the door and Clint peeked inside. "Hey, we better get this show on the road. I hear the groom is about to split."

Meg stuck her tongue out at her brother. He looked so handsome in his dove gray tuxedo. His sandy-colored hair had been cut and styled for the occasion. Clint might only be twenty-one, but for so many years he'd had to handle a lot of responsibility, and he'd done a good job. Her nineteen-year-old brother, Rick, appeared behind Clint's shoulders. He, too, looked handsome as he politely offered his arm to escort Nikki. Meg ached to tell everyone the truth. The family resemblance between Nikki and Rick was amazing. Both had inherited their mother's dark hair and coloring.

"You about ready, sis?" Clint asked.

"What?" Meg shook her head. "Oh, sure."

Her brother raised an eyebrow. "You okay?"

"Of course. Just a little nervous."

Her brother didn't look convinced. He moved closer when Nikki and Rick left the room. "Look, Meg, if you're having second thoughts. I mean, if you're in trouble, I want you to know that you can always come back home to Rick and me. We'll take care of you."

Meg's mouth dropped open. Clint thought she might be pregnant! It was a natural assumption, she supposed. She had left home nearly three months ago, planning to take the big city by storm, and instead she was rushing into marriage with a horse rancher. And whether he liked it or not, she loved the man.

She placed a kiss on Clint's cheek. Nikki meant as much to Linc as Meg's brothers meant to her, and that was the only reason Linc Stoner was marrying her today. She had to remember that, as much as it hurt. "It's sweet of you to care so much, but you're not going to be an uncle any time soon." A brother, yes, she thought. "And yes, this is what I want."

"Okay then. Let's go." He finally smiled as she took his arm and they headed downstairs. Yes, she was doing the right thing, she kept repeating to herself as they made their way through the house. Once they stepped out on the patio the music changed and the wedding party started down the aisle.

Everyone stood, and Clint covered her hand with his. Panic hit her hard and she had the urge to run, until she spotted Linc. He looked wonderful in his tux, with his black hair combed back neatly except for a few wayward strands that fell onto his forehead. She caught the tender gaze in his dark eyes and felt, at that moment, that everything was going to work out fine. They walked up the aisle, and when her brother placed her hand in Linc's, she knew she wasn't going anywhere.

To Linc's relief, the wedding vows took only a few minutes. Once the minister announced they were husband and wife, Linc turned to kiss his bride and the crowd erupted with applause. The next thing he knew, everyone was slapping him on the back in congratulations.

When the reception began, the champagne started to flow, and the next two hours were a blur. Well-meaning friends toasted them a few dozen times, and with Meg at his side, Linc handled all the teasing remarks about married life.

Luckily, by seven o'clock Linc's head had cleared enough to drive. He helped Meg into the car. She said goodbye to her brothers and promised Nikki they'd be back in a few days. Then Linc kissed his sister and warned her to behave for Beth and Dave, who planned to stay until the bride and groom returned from the honeymoon.

Linc started the engine and they drove away under a shower of rice. He sighed in relief. "Jeez, I thought we'd never get out of there," he muttered as they drove under the archway and pulled out onto the highway.

Meg looked out the window. "It was good seeing my brothers again. I've missed them."

Linc reached across the car and took her hand in his. "Meg, I know this is going to be hard for a while, but you can visit your brothers any time you want, just maybe not at the ranch. Someone might notice how much Rick and Nikki...."

"Oh," Meg said. "You saw the resemblance, too?"

"Yeah," he said. "Do you think Clint and Rick noticed?"

Meg began to realize just how difficult it would be to keep the secret about Nikki's origins from her brothers. Oh, Mama, what have you done to me? she thought. "I doubt it."

"Well, you can go visit them in Oklahoma."

"Things are different now," she said softly.

"You mean because we're married."

She nodded.

"Look, I'm not going to keep you under lock and key." He gave her a sideways glance. "Is that what you're afraid of?"

Meg folded her arms. "I wouldn't let you if you tried."

Linc cursed and pulled to the side of the road. He threw the car into park and turned to her. "Listen here. I'm not my old man. I don't go around beating women and children."

Her mouth dropped open. "Oh, Linc. I never thought that. You've been nothing but kind and gentle with me." She turned away. "But my dad ruled my mother's life so completely. She was afraid to open her mouth around him. I will never allow that to happen to me."

He reached for her and pulled her across the front seat. She gasped in surprise as she ended up on his lap. "Meg, I promise I will never force you to do anything you don't want to."

She was so close to him she could feel his breath on her face. "I know you won't, Linc. I trust you."

He placed a soft kiss on her lips, then another. All at once the temperature in the car started to heat up. "You might not say that if you knew what was on my mind right now."

Meg met his smoldering gaze and felt her own pulse racing. "Would you be shocked if I told you that I've been thinking the same—"

His mouth covered hers, swallowing up the rest of her words. But that didn't bother Meg. She slipped her arms around his neck and pressed her body against his, returning his kiss. He groaned and parted her lips with his tongue, stroking hers hungrily.

"Lord, Meg. I want you so much." He leaned his head against hers and drew a long breath. "But if we don't stop this we're going to end up making love in the car. And I want to make your first time special."

"With you it's bound to be special," she said shyly.

He groaned again and lifted her off his lap and back into her seat. "Just stay there until we get to the hotel." He threw the car into drive. The wheels squealed as he took off down the highway. "Hopefully we'll be there soon." He took a frank and admiring look at her. "Real soon."

The bellman carried their bags up to the suite at the Hotel Crescent Court in downtown Dallas. Meg busied herself looking around the beautiful surroundings, but her gaze kept wandering toward the bedroom, and suddenly she was nervous all over again.

She heard the door close and realized she and Linc were alone. He came up behind her and placed a feathery kiss on her neck. She jumped.

"Calm down, darlin'," he said. "I was going to suggest we go down and get some dinner. I noticed you didn't eat much at the wedding."

"I am hungry," she lied, glad for the distraction. "Just let me freshen up."

Meg grabbed her overnight bag and went into the bathroom, where she splashed cold water on her face and applied some lipstick. She took a calming breath and glanced down at the gold band on her finger. It was hard to believe she was married. She was Mrs. Linc Stoner. She loved him, more than she had thought it was possible, but she mustn't forget why he had married her.

Only for Nikki. That thought echoed inside her head.

They went downstairs and Linc escorted her into the hotel restaurant. A waiter showed them to a small table off by themselves and Meg felt so special as she walked along with her arm through Linc's. Once seated across from her new husband, he ordered a bottle of wine and the waiter left them alone.

"I hope you like this place. I know the food is good."

"It's lovely," Meg managed, wondering when Linc had been here before, and with whom.

Linc reached across the table and took her hand. "Good. And this meal is going to be just the beginning of a wonderful honeymoon."

The waiter returned with the wine. After pouring them each a glass, Linc raised his toward her.

"To my beautiful bride," he said

"Thank you." Meg blushed. She'd never had a man call her beautiful before. Did he mean it? Surely Linc had gone out with a lot of beautiful women.

Their meal was slow and easy, filled with conversation about what there was to see and do in Dallas. After her second glass of champagne, Meg felt her nervousness fading. They finished dinner, toured the hotel lobby and shops, stopped by the bar to listen to the band play. He surprised her by asking her to dance when a soft ballad filled the air. Meg nodded, but when he took her into his arms, she was lost. He wrapped his arm around her back, drawing her close, so close her breasts were crushed against his chest. His leg moved between hers, causing a hot friction through the delicate material of her dress. He raised his head, and his nearly black eyes locked with hers, relaying his desire.

"I haven't danced in a long time," he whispered.

Meg couldn't remember ever dancing with a man. Not like this, anyway. "It's been a long time for me, too."

He placed his forehead against hers and lifted her hand to his shoulder. "I guess we'll just have to do it more often."

"I'd like that." She closed her eyes and let the music take her. She and Linc were the only two people in the world. Finally the song ended and he escorted her off the floor and out of the bar. Silently, they rode the elevator upstairs to their room. When the door closed, he pulled Meg into his arms, and she went willingly.

Linc's mouth covered hers, and he had difficulty convincing himself that he didn't care passionately for this woman. So why had he been so patient with her? He told himself he was only ensuring his link to Nikki. But the fact remained that Meg was in his arms, her shapely body pressed against his hungry one, and the thought flashed though his mind that he wanted her in his life. Maybe forever.

She tasted warm and rich, like everything he ever wanted, like everything he ever hoped to find in a woman. He picked her up and carried her into the dimly lit bedroom, where he set her down on the king-size bed. That's when he felt her tremble, heard her sharp intake of breath, knew he was rushing her. With the last shred of willpower he released her and stepped back.

"I think it might be a good idea if we call it a night."

The dim light in the room was enough to allow him to see her shocked expression. "But I thought you wanted…"

He placed his finger over her lips. "I do want you, Megan Stoner. But I also know I rushed you into this marriage. And I won't rush you into bed. You need time, Meg. And I'm going to give you as much as you need. No pressure. When you decide the time is right, you come to me."

Her eyes were big and round. Her luscious mouth was

parted slightly, begging him to take little nibbling bits, but he resisted.

"When you're ready, you come to me," he repeated. He backed out of the room, hoping that she'd ask him to stay. He was more than disappointed when she didn't, but he'd survive. He looked at the sofa and groaned. He stripped out of his shirt and hung it over the chair. Sitting down, he pulled off his boots. Then came his pants. Stripped to his underwear, he lay down on the sofa and punched one of the toss pillows and placed it under his head, then he stretched his long legs over the edge. This certainly wasn't how he'd envisioned spending his wedding night.

The next morning Meg woke early as usual, but she hadn't slept well. She sat up, suddenly remembering where she was and that she was in this big elegant bed...alone. Linc had decided to sleep elsewhere. Trying not to think about that, she got up and went to the bathroom, but when she pushed the door open she discovered her husband standing at the sink, shaving. Her eyes quickly scanned his near-naked body. Only a towel draped around his hips kept his modesty intact.

He turned and smiled at her. "Good morning." He leaned toward her and placed a quick kiss on her surprised mouth. "I hope you had a good night."

"It was fine," she lied.

He ran the razor over his cheek, then turned back to her, his gaze concentrating on the white satin gown that Nikki had insisted Meg needed for her wedding night. Oh, sure, some wedding night. But she did get a little satisfaction out of seeing Linc's eyes nearly pop out of their sockets.

"Nice gown," he commented, his voice husky.

She felt flirtatious and turned around to model it. "Thank you. You bought it for me."

He picked up a towel and wiped the remaining shaving cream off his face. "I have great taste."

"Yes, you do," Meg said. But when Linc came toward her she thought she might have gone too far. "If you're finished with the bathroom, maybe I should get dressed."

He tossed her that grin she was so crazy about. "We could share," he offered.

"I think I'll wait."

Before she could get away, he grabbed her and pulled her against his bare chest. She gasped as his mouth closed over hers and began working its magic. She came alive in his arms. She wrapped her arms around his neck and returned his kiss. Then he released her. "Get dressed and we'll go down for breakfast, then go see some of Dallas." He brushed past her, grabbed his suitcase and carried it into the other room, leaving her all alone.

It didn't look like sleeping on the sofa bothered Linc that much. Well, it didn't bother her either. She closed the bedroom door and pulled out a skirt and a cotton shirt to wear today. She went into the bathroom and turned on the shower. She removed her beautiful gown, vowing that the next time she wore it, she wouldn't be sleeping alone.

The day grew warm rapidly. After breakfast, they'd spent the rest of the morning shopping in the hotel's elegant stores. Linc insisted on buying Meg a new swimsuit. She refused at first, but he said he was her husband and therefore allowed to buy her things.

Meg finally agreed. But modeling suits for Linc made her nervous. There was no denying the desire she saw in his eyes. They both decided on a one-piece teal blue suit with French-cut legs, and while she changed, Linc bought the matching cover-up and a suit for himself.

Meg found a bright pink sundress for Nikki, and they purchased that too. After taking their packages up to their room, they quickly changed into their new swim clothes and had lunch by the hotel pool. They spent a few hours just relaxing in the sun, but only after Linc made sure his new wife was well covered with sunscreen. Meg happily returned the favor as she rubbed the lotion over his warm back.

It had been a wonderful afternoon. Linc had now taken her to the only exciting places she'd ever been—San Antonio and Dallas. Later that night they went out for dinner at a Mexican restaurant downtown. They listened to mariachi music awhile drinking margaritas. By the time they returned to the hotel it was after midnight.

Meg floated into the room, still humming along with the music in her head. "Oh, Linc, I had such a lovely evening. It's been a perfect day."

Linc watched Meg and could only smile, knowing he had never seen her so relaxed. They'd had a great time together. He wished he could make it a perfect night, as well. Something was happening between them, but he knew it wasn't just the growing sexual tension. He was beginning to think this marriage of theirs might just make it off the ground. Just give it time, he ordered himself.

He tossed the room key on the table. "I'll call the concierge the first thing in the morning and see if he has any suggestions on how to spend tomorrow." He looked at her across the room and all at once he ached for her. He would sell his soul to have her in his arms tonight.

"I guess I better get some sleep if we're getting up early." She started for the bedroom and he had to stop himself from calling her back.

"Sounds like a good idea."

Meg stopped at the bedroom door. "Good night, Linc."

"Night, Meg."

She held his dark gaze as her heart pounded in her chest. Please don't make me leave, she cried silently. But finally he turned away and she had no choice but to go into the bedroom.

She hung up her dress and stepped out of her heels. Once out of her underwear, she put on her gown and sat down on the edge of the bed. Now what? Meg glanced around the room. She could watch television or read, but she didn't want to do either. She wanted Linc. Her insides were going crazy. Her heart was pounding like a hammer against her ribs.

But from the look of things, if she didn't do something about it, nothing was going to get done. She stood and walked to the door. She drew a long breath and leaned against it. No, she couldn't go in there. What if he changed his mind...about wanting her?

Suddenly there was a knock on the door. She gasped and jerked it open to find Linc standing there in his black jeans, but shirtless. He was holding his shaving kit.

"If you're finished, do you think I could use the bathroom. I feel like a shower."

Meg stood there staring at his chest, aching to run her hands through the dark hair. "Sure."

He stepped past her and went into the bathroom and closed the door. She sank onto the bed. She couldn't handle this. She loved this man, but hesitated to tell him that she wanted him to make love to her. Why? He'd been honest with her. He wanted her, but didn't love her. Could she settle for that? It didn't seem to be her choice anymore. Her heart had overruled her common sense. She wanted to be Linc Stoner's wife—a real wife. There was no way she was going to spend one more night alone.

She listened to the sound of the shower, and suddenly the water stopped. After a few minutes the door opened and he came out.

"Thanks," he said as he walked past her. He looked so sexy. All warm and clean.

Without thinking, Meg grabbed his arm to stop him. "Please don't go," she implored.

Linc stared down at her hand, then up into her eyes. "What is it, Meg?"

She swallowed. "I want you to make love to me."

"Oh, darlin', are you sure?"

She nodded. "Yes."

Linc didn't know if he was dreaming. He didn't care, just so long as he didn't wake up. He dropped his towel, and his mouth quickly took her in a searing kiss as he pulled her against him.

He realized how anxious he was and forced himself to slow down. "You look so beautiful in this gown." He reached for the straps and began to slip them from her shoulders. "Maybe we should take it off so it won't get damaged." He exposed her breasts and closed his eyes momentarily. "Oh, Meg." His hand trembled as he cupped the delicate weight in his palm.

When Meg's shaky hands found his chest, he let go with a throaty groan. He had thought he'd known what it was to want someone, to ache with hunger, but nothing had ever compared to this, no dream or fantasy.

He felt her tremble and he turned hard with desire. She was small and fragile, her slender frame tucked against his. But he knew her strength and determination, and admired her for both. He wanted this woman. Wanted her now! He pulled her tightly against him, closed his mouth over hers, and everything seemed to spin out of control.

Meg started to lose all thought as soon as she touched Linc's heated skin. She couldn't think, she could only react. There was nothing else in the world but this man whom she loved so desperately. She clung to him, holding on as if he were her lifeline, the desire spreading through her veins. She'd known Linc for such a short time, but he'd stolen her heart and she wanted to be with him for as long as he wanted her.

He broke off the kiss and stared down into her brown eyes, those eyes that boldly revealed her need and desire for him. Her arms went around his neck, her sweet breath moved against his face. "Make love to me, Linc."

His mouth whispered against hers, "It'll be my pleasure, Mrs. Stoner." His hands stroked the gown down over her creamy hips and thighs, then he helped her step out of it. After feasting on her, he placed her down on the bed.

"You're beautiful," he groaned. "Don't move. I'll be right back."

He quickly removed his clothes, then went into the other room and pulled a foil packet from his shaving kit. Rushing back, he tossed it on the nightstand, knelt down on the mattress and placed a kiss on Meg's lips. Her mouth was so soft, so giving and willing, her tongue dancing against his own. A fire caught inside him as he threaded his finger through her golden hair.

"Ah, Meg," he said, and shifted until he was nearly on top of her. He kissed her chin, lingering, tasting the tip with his tongue, moving downward to her neck, the whispers of her perfume nearly driving him crazy. His lips caressed the swell of her breasts and he felt her shudder. Linc closed his eyes, moving his face against her heated skin, reveling in the supple flesh. His lips sucked one nipple into a tight bud, and she rewarded him with a hungry cry and pushed her hips against him.

"Linc!" she gasped his name, her hands gripping his shoulders. "Please."

"Tell me what you want, darlin'."

Meg wasn't sure. The only thing she knew was she wanted Linc to stop the delicious ache between her legs. "Make love to me." Trembling uncontrollably, she opened herself to him.

Linc's mouth captured hers as his hand reached between them and began stroking her.

"It's going to hurt a little," he said as he moved over her and began to push against her. She saw the intensity on his face, and knew he was holding back for her. It only made her love him more. She raised her hips and a sharp pain took her, then it quickly disappeared as Linc buried himself inside her. Her cry was a combination of pain and pleasure.

For an instant Linc paused, reveling in the feel of her around him. Then he began to move in slow, deep strokes, wanting the intensity to last. He brushed her mouth with his, thrilled to watch Meg's expression, seeing her desire build as her legs tangled around his, her body tensed and heated.

Their movement grew fierce, their breathing ragged, their skin brushing, touching, until he thought he would die from the pleasure. Then Meg came apart in his arms. A long, low cry escaped her throat and Linc couldn't control his movements any longer. He finally gave in, throwing his head back and groaning her name. Then he buried his face against her neck.

Meg never dreamed passion could be like this. Her arms held the man she loved tightly against her. She could still feel the final tremors in his body, and they thrilled her.

Linc raised his head. He brushed her hair from her face. "You okay, darlin'?"

Meg nodded. "I'm fine." She smiled shyly. "I'm better than fine. I'm wonderful."

"I'm glad." He kissed her on the lips, then moved off her, pulling her against his side. "I feel pretty good myself."

"So I didn't disappoint you?"

Linc looked at her. "You had me half-crazy before I even climbed into this bed." He reached across her to the nightstand and held up the foil packet. "So crazy I forgot this."

They had a wonderful time in Dallas, but it was time they headed back to the ranch. During the ride home Meg reflected on the past three days. Three wonderful days. She was happier than she'd ever been, and Linc couldn't have been more attentive to her. She felt herself blush just thinking about how unbelievably tender he'd been, how he'd also managed to bring out the wanton in her. She smiled, remembering the night before and how she'd seduced her husband into—

"Hey, it better be me who's causing that big smile." He reached over and took her hand as they drove back to the ranch.

"If you must know, it is. Thank you for the wonderful weekend."

He brought her fingers to his lips and pressed a kiss against her skin. A shiver rushed though her. Would she always react to this man with such excitement?

"I'm hoping it will be for more that just a weekend." He cocked an eyebrow. "You're my wife, Meg. When we get home, I want you to move into my bedroom."

Meg swallowed, thrilled at his words. "I'd like that, too." She scooted across the seat and put her arms around his neck. "I like sharing your bed," she breathed against his ear. Suddenly the car swerved to the side of the two-lane road. Linc pushed the gearshift into park and yanked Meg onto his lap. She gasped, but his mouth smothered her words with a hungry kiss as his hands roamed under her sweater, finding her breasts.

He broke off the kiss and began taking small nibbles along her lower lip. "How do you feel about making love under a tree alongside the road?"

She shivered. "If you're in the mood."

"With you I always seem to be in the mood. I have a feeling that my workday is going to be shortened considerably."

Meg kissed him. "We'll have to be careful. There's a teenager in the house."

He groaned. "We'll just send her to bed early, and put locks on all the doors so we can have some privacy."

"Linc, we can't do that. Nikki needs us."

"Meg, I need you."

She'd rather hear the word *love,* but need was enough for now. She had to realize that this might be all she was going to get. She scooted off his lap and straightened her dark slacks and blouse. "You're going to have to wait until tonight. We promised everyone we would be home in time for dinner. Dora is fixing us a special meal."

"Okay, but we're retiring early, being that we're so tired from our long trip." He winked, making Meg regret those lost minutes under that tree.

Her hand touched his arm and he looked at her. She drew a breath to slow her rapid heart. "Promise me that you'll take me to that tree someday soon."

"Darlin', anytime. But first I plan on initiating the pool." A slow grin spread across his handsome face. "Can't tell you how many fantasies I've had about you since the first time I saw you there." His expression grew serious and he cupped her face. "At first I thought I was dreaming. You were simply the most beautiful creature I'd ever seen." He gave her a quick, hard kiss. "Later," he promised, then put the car into drive and moved back onto the road.

Meg was smiling as they headed home. She had already begun to think of the ranch as her home. She glanced across the front seat. And of Linc as her husband...for however long it would be.

Their car came to a stop in front of the house, and Nikki was the first one out the door to greet them. She came flying off the porch and into Linc's arms.

"What a welcome," he said, enjoying the smile on his sister's face. "Maybe I should leave more often."

"No, you can't. You have a wife now."

Linc grabbed Meg and pulled her to his side, then placed a kiss on her cute smiling mouth. Damn! He already wanted her again. "I guess I'm stuck here on the ranch for the rest of my days."

Meg jabbed him in the ribs. "Ouch. That hurt."

"Then watch your mouth," Meg ordered, smiling.

Linc leaned toward his wife and whispered in her ear, telling her he planned to do more than watch mouths when they were alone.

"Hey, the newlyweds have returned," Dave said as he came down the steps. Close behind was Beth. "Welcome home." They exchanged hugs with everyone.

"Come on in the house, son," Dave suggested. "Beth and Dora have cooked us a feast."

Meg hung back with Nikki. "I'm so glad you're home," Nikki began. "I really missed you."

Meg hugged her sister. "I missed you, too."

"How could you? You were on your honeymoon." Nikki's eyes lit up. "Is my brother real romantic?"

Meg was taken aback by the question and felt herself blush. "Yes, Linc can be very romantic."

"Does that mean you two are going to have a baby?"

Meg's mouth dropped open. "Nikki. That's something that's private between your brother and me." Meg couldn't help but recall that the first time they made love they hadn't used protection. "Remember, we've only been married a few days."

"I know, but having a family would be so neat. Julie has two brothers and one sister."

You do, too, Meg almost cried. Instead, she put her arm around her sister and together they started up to the porch. "You have Linc and now me."

"I know. And I love it that you married Linc, but...but I want to find out about my real family." The thirteen-year-old stopped and looked at Meg. "When my mom and daddy were alive, I didn't want to hurt their feelings, but now that they're gone, do you think you can help me find my biological mother and father?"

Meg's heart pounded so hard in her chest, she thought the world could hear it. She glanced over Nikki's shoulder just in time to see Linc disappear into the house with Beth and Dave.

"Don't you think Linc is the one you should be talking to about this? He is your brother and legal guardian."

Nikki stomped her foot. "He won't do it. He doesn't think it's important. Just because his dad was rotten, he thinks that all of the people who give their children up for adoption are."

Meg tried to control her shakiness. "You don't resent your biological parents...for giving you up?"

Nikki looked thoughtful. "I don't know. I'd like to think that my real mother loved me so much that she thought she was doing what was best for me."

Meg smiled at her sister and hugged her. *Oh, Nikki,* she cried silently. *Your mother loved you more than you'll ever know. And I promise someday I'll tell you and you'll know all about her.*

Chapter Nine

It was well after midnight when Meg came out of Nikki's room. The thirteen-year-old didn't need checking on, but Meg did it anyway. Nikki was her responsibility now, and the thought warmed Meg's heart. If only she could tell her they were truly sisters.

After closing Nikki's door, Meg tiptoed past the guest room where Dave and Beth were staying and continued on down the hall to her bedroom. Suddenly she was grabbed from behind.

"You're headin' the wrong way, darlin'," Linc said as he tossed her over his shoulder and turned toward the master bedroom.

"Put me down," Meg gasped in a whispered voice, afraid of waking up everyone in the house.

"Just as soon as you're where you belong." He opened the door to his bedroom and set her down on her feet.

Meg's head was still spinning as she jammed her hands on her hips and glared at her husband's cocky grin. "How dare you..." she began, but lost her train of thought as she noticed her surroundings. The room had been done in shades of brown and tan. The thick carpeting under her feet was a buckskin color, bringing out the rich color of the oak furniture. Eggshell-colored walls were nearly bare except for a huge Southwestern painting hanging over a large brass bed.

Linc cocked an eyebrow. "You like?"

"It's beautiful." She jerked around to Linc. "But that doesn't give you the right to manhandle me."

He sobered. "You're my wife, Meg. I thought you wanted to be in my bed."

"If you'd given me a few minutes I would have been." She pointed in the direction of her old room. "All my clothes are down the hall..." Her voice drifted off as her eyes were drawn to a large bed cover with a hand-sewn wedding quilt. "I was just getting something to sleep in. Oh, Linc, it's lovely."

He came up behind her and took her into his arms. "Glad you like it. The bed belonged to my parents. Before we left for Dallas, I asked Dave to have it brought down from the attic. The quilt is one Pauline made."

Linc had done this for her? Tears welled in Meg's eyes as her fingers drifted over the beautiful comforter. She'd never in her life felt so special.

He turned her in his arms. "Now, since when did you need something to sleep in?"

She felt her face heat up, unable to forget their weekend together in Dallas. They'd spent hours in bed making love.

"For that matter, who's going to be sleeping?"

"I just thought with so many people in the house it might be better if..."

Linc walked to the door and secured the lock. "This was how my parents got privacy." He came back and started nuzzling her neck. "I can't tell you how many times I heard that lock click."

"Linc," she gasped, from the sensation he was creating. "There's a thirteen-year-old in the house, we can't just—"

Her words were cut off when his mouth covered hers. The hungry kiss soon had Meg forgetting her concerns as his body moved against hers. Then he went to work stripping off her clothes. She, too, got involved by helping Linc pull down his jeans, but soon discovered that the boots had to come off first.

Once naked, they fell onto the bed laughing. The laughter died away when Linc's hands and mouth set them both on fire, and soon they were both breathing in pants and gasps. Finally he filled her and the pleasure spiraled through her. Her body strained to his, moving with his tempo until everything exploded around them. She bit back the words of love she ached to say as Linc silently pulled her to his side, his hand draped over her waist, holding her close against him.

They lay quietly together for a few minutes, savoring the closeness. This was all so perfect. The last thing Meg wanted to do was spoil the afterglow of their wonderful lovemaking, but they had to discuss Nikki.

"Linc, we need to talk about Nikki," Meg finally said.

"Sure, honey," he mumbled, and kissed the back of her neck.

"When we got home today, she was so happy about us getting married."

Linc squeezed her. "I know, honey."

"But I think she's still having problems. I think she might be afraid she won't fit in." Meg pulled the blanket up over them. "She asked me to help her...help her find her birth parents." Meg bit her lip, waiting for Linc's reaction, but it never came. All she heard was the soft sound of his peaceful snoring.

He'd fallen asleep. She started to shake him, then realized it was after one o'clock. They both had to get up in a few hours. Maybe it would be better if she waited to tell him about Nikki's request. She snuggled against her husband's warmth and pretended for a while that things were perfect.

The next morning, breakfast was hectic as Dave and Beth got ready to head back to their ranch. There wasn't a chance for Meg to talk privately with Linc.

After being gone for nearly four days, Linc had a lot of work ahead of him. He said his goodbyes to Beth and Dave, then walked Meg out the door onto the porch so they could have time alone. He pulled her into his arms and captured her mouth in a long, sensual kiss. By the time he pulled away, she could barely stand on her own.

"That's gonna have to hold me until supper."

"Why supper?"

"Sorry, darlin'." He tipped his hat back off his forehead. "I forgot to tell you. Dale and I have to deliver a mare over by Crowley." He touched her nose with a finger and smiled. "Gonna miss me?"

She nodded, knowing she'd think about him constantly until he returned.

"On second thought, I think I need another one to hold me over." He bent his head and covered her willing mouth. Before long, Meg was clinging to him, returning the kiss.

He released her. "I promise, Meg, I'll make leaving now up to you tonight," he whispered, then strode off toward the barn.

Her heart in her throat, Meg watched the man she loved walk away. She ached to call him back, to hide in the safety of his arms and pretend for a while longer there weren't any problems. To pretend he married her because he loved her, not because he needed her to help with raising Nikki.

"It's tough watching them go off."

Meg turned to find Beth on the porch. "Oh, hi. I didn't see you."

The older woman smiled. "I know. You can't concentrate on anything but your man. Love will do that to ya." Beth studied her for a moment. "I'm so glad Linc found you. He deserves some happiness."

Meg's gaze followed Linc until he disappeared into the barn.

"He had wounds, bad ones, that took a long time to heal," Beth went on. "Both physical and emotional. When Joe brought him into the family, it was almost as if Linc was afraid to take their love. Pauline used to worry about him, wondering if Linc would ever accept her and Joe. It wasn't until Nikki arrived that Linc began to change. He's always been crazy about that girl."

"I know." Meg had always known that about Linc. Even if things didn't work out between them, she knew that Nikki would have all the love she needed.

"Now he's in love with you."

Meg's head jerked around, her heart pounding with hope. If only that were true.

"A man like Linc doesn't give his love easily, but when he does, it's for keeps. He's a good man." Beth brushed Meg's braid off her shoulder. "But stepping into a ready-made family can be difficult. If you ever need to talk about Nikki or about anything, don't hesitate to call me."

Meg wanted desperately to confess her secret to Beth. But all she could do was nod and hug her new friend. "Thanks for watching Nikki and helping out here."

"It was our pleasure. Now it's your turn to come visit us."

"We will."

Dave came out the door carrying two suitcases and put them into the back of their Suburban. "Just make sure you do. I want to hear all about Starfire."

Meg smiled at the mention of the ranch's future stud. "I don't think you have to worry about that. Linc is so excited, he made a special trip out to the barn last night."

Dave kissed her cheek. "Yeah, but you're the only filly on Linc's mind these days," he teased, then helped his wife into the car. Meg stood on the porch and waved as they drove off.

Still smiling, she turned to go into the house.

Despite the warmth of the day, Meg shivered. The last few days had seemed almost too wonderful. Too wonderful to last.

Linc was busy helping Dale hook up the horse trailer when Nikki appeared.

"Need any help?" she asked.

"Nope, we got it now," Linc said as he pulled off his work gloves. "It was a stubborn hitch."

The teenager kicked at the dirt, as if she had something else to say. She was dressed in jeans, a checkered blouse and her favorite riding boots. He had to smile. His sister was looking like she used to. He also knew from experience that she wanted something.

"What's on your mind?" he asked when Dale disappeared into the barn.

"What makes you think I've got something on my mind?"

He cocked an eyebrow. "I know you."

"Can I go with you and Dale today?" she asked. "I promise that I won't cause any trouble. I want to get out of here for a while."

Linc knew summer school didn't start until next week, but he was still surprised Nikki wanted to spend the day riding in a truck cab. More than likely she wanted to spend time with Dale. His sister had had a crush on the ranch foreman since he helped her with her horse nearly three years ago. It had been cute when she was ten, but at thirteen the thought made him nervous. Nikki being with any male made him nervous.

"Don't you have a counseling appointment this afternoon?"

She glanced away. "Can't I miss this once?"

He walked around the back of the trailer and pulled out the ramp as Dale led the chestnut mare out of the barn. "I don't think it's a good idea, Nik."

"Why not?" the thirteen-year-old whined. "I never go anywhere anymore. Now that you're married you'll probably forget all about me."

Linc put his hands on his hips and stared, unbelieving, at his sister. Hell, wasn't that the reason he'd gotten married? To give his sister a stable home. "You honestly believe that?"

Nikki toyed with her dark hair and shrugged. "Well, we used to do a lot of things together."

"The last few months you haven't been able to stand the sight of me."

She glanced away. "That's because I blamed you for what happened."

He didn't need to hear this. He still hadn't forgiven himself for what had happened to Joe and Pauline.

"I don't anymore," Nikki continued. "Dr. Kathy said that I was striking out at you because I felt safe taking my anger out on you." She looked away shyly. "Because I knew you loved me…no matter what."

Linc didn't care about the explanation as much as the fact that he was just happy she didn't hate him anymore. He swallowed back the huge lump in his throat. "That will never change, Nik."

She gave him a nod. "I'm sorry I caused you so much trouble." Tears filled her eyes.

Linc's heart soared. He had his Nikki back. "Well, you try it again and you're gonna get smacked on the seat of your jeans." He swatted at her with his gloves.

She giggled "Yeah, sure. You've never spanked me ever."

"And that's the reason you're a spoiled brat."

"And you love me to pieces."

Linc tipped the brim of his hat off his forehead, hearing Nikki repeat the childhood phrase he used to recite to her. "No matter what, Nikki, I will always love you to pieces."

She went into his arms. "Oh, Linc, I love you, too."

He closed his eyes and savored the rare moment with his sister. It had been so long since she'd been this loving.

She pulled away from him just as Dale latched the trailer gate. "Ready, boss."

"Now can I go with you?" she asked.

Linc studied her for a moment. He really hadn't spent much time with her lately. In fact, not since the accident. Sharing a day together might be good for both of them. "You've got five minutes before we pull out."

A big smile lit up the girl's face. "I'm ready now." She ran around to the passenger side of the truck. "Oh, can you tell Meg?"

"You stinker. You're leaving me to do the dirty work."

"Please. She'll say yes if you ask."

"And she'll take it out of my hide," he murmured as he walked past his foreman to use the phone in the tack room.

"It's a good thing for you Meg loves your old hide," Dale called after him.

If that were only true, Linc thought as he walked into the barn.

Meg paced the bedroom floor, then stopped to glance out the window to see if Linc and Nikki had returned yet. There was no truck coming up the road. She checked her watch. It was nearly eight o'clock. Even though she'd gotten a call from Linc three hours ago explaining they were running late, Meg wasn't happy. Nikki never should have been allowed to go in the first place. Linc knew that. What upset her the most was that he'd let Nikki manipulate him again.

Meg grabbed a towel out of the cupboard and headed downstairs to the patio. The last thing she wanted was for Linc to know that she had been sitting around all night, waiting for him to come home. Turning on the pool lights, she tossed her towel on the chair and went to the edge of the pool. After pulling her hair back into a ponytail, she dove into the cool, clear water.

Still underwater, she pushed all the way to the shallow end. Then, feeling her lungs about to burst from lack of oxygen, she surfaced with a gasp. She began swimming laps, wondering if this was how things were going to be between her and her husband.

So far, Linc had been calling all the shots. Nothing in his life seemed to have changed. What had he given up since this...this so-called marriage took place? Nothing, except he had to share his bed. And that didn't seem such a hardship.

He was determined to have his own way, and what could she say about it? She had no right to demand he spend all his time with her, especially if he didn't want to. That hurt. They were married only a little over a week, and he'd been gone all day and most of the evening. Guess she wasn't as irresistible as she thought. She was even more irritated that she had missed him. She continued to slash through the water, her arms beginning to ache, but she ignored the pain and turned at the end of the pool and started back. Finally she had exhausted her anger and her strength. She clung to the ledge and wiped the water from her face.

"I was wondering when you were going to wear yourself out."

Meg gasped as she looked up to find Linc sitting in a chair. He was still dressed in the jeans and boots he wore out of the house that morning. He pulled his hat off, showing his sexy grin. She glanced away, already feeling a stirring low in her stomach. Damn the man! All he had to do was smile and she melted inside.

"I was just getting some exercise before I turned in," she said.

"You should have waited for me."

She glared at him. "And just how was I to know when you would get home?"

"I called and said we'd be late."

"Nearly four hours ago," she reminded him.

"Three," he corrected. Linc studied her for a moment. He loved seeing that fiery glint in her eyes. "You missed me?" he teased.

She shrugged those lovely bare shoulders of hers. "I hardly noticed you were gone."

Like hell! he thought as he began pulling off his boots, all the while keeping his gaze on Meg, watching as her eyes grew large with curiosity. Next he tugged his shirt from the waistband of his jeans.

"What are doing?"

He stood and tossed his shirt on the chair. "I'm goin' for a swim."

"But you don't have a suit."

He placed his hand on his hips. "My getting naked bother you?"

"No." Meg turned toward the doors. "But what if Nikki comes down?"

Silently, Linc stripped off his jeans and underwear and walked to the shallow end of the pool. "Nikki has strict instructions to stay in her room for the rest of the night. I told her I wanted some private time with my wife."

Meg's throat went dry as she looked up at her gloriously naked husband. Her heart soared as he came down the steps and into the water.

"Meg, I'm real sorry I didn't get home sooner. You

gotta know that I'd rather be with you than a couple of old horse breeders.''

Her eyes met his. "Really?"

"Let's see. How can I convince you?" Linc reached for her and pulled her against him. Then his mouth closed over hers. Meg's hands moved up his chest and circled his neck, welcoming him home. This was where she wanted to be— in his arms...in his life...permanently.

But realistically, how long would her happiness last? How long would she be Linc's wife? No matter how great the sex was between them, it wasn't love. And as much as she loved Linc, he didn't return those feelings. Meg doubted their marriage could survive. She'd do anything to keep her new family together. But their happiness was based on a lie. A lie that could rip them apart.

Soon Linc had her suit pulled down and Meg was powerless to deny him anything. Tomorrow. She would wait until tomorrow and talk to him about the situation. There was no room in her head right now for problems, only for loving her man.

Most every morning Linc and Meg shared breakfast together. After a while Dora even left them so they could be alone. And Meg liked that just fine, since her husband couldn't seem to keep his hands off her.

"Would you stop?" Meg pushed him away. "Dora might come in."

"She'll think it's strange that you and I are kissing?" He shrugged. "I guess if it bothers you, I just might have to stop."

Meg grabbed her husband by the arm before he got away. "Don't you dare." She gave him a long, thorough kiss.

Linc's nearly black eyes smoldered with desire. "This can get pretty addictive, huh?"

Meg nodded, but before she could say anything, they

heard Nikki coming down the stairs. She walked into the kitchen, smiling. "Hi, guys."

"You're awfully cheerful."

"Well, I only have a few days of freedom left before summer school starts, so I thought I'd spend it today working with Sweetie."

Linc exchanged a quick glance with Meg. "Sounds like a good idea, but I believe you have an appointment this afternoon with your counselor."

"Darn!" The girl dropped into her chair. "I forgot. I wanted to go riding with Julie." She looked hopefully at Meg. "Do you think you can change—"

Meg shook her head. "You were lucky they had a cancelation for today to replace the appointment you broke yesterday."

"Well, I don't need those stupid sessions anyway. Why do I still have to go?"

Linc spoke up. "Because the court said so."

"But I'm okay now."

"And let's keep it that way." Linc stood, walked around the table and kissed his sister, then stopped at Meg. He bent down and kissed her long and hard, finally pulling away. "I'll see you at lunch," he promised, and was out the door.

Meg watched him until he disappeared.

Nikki leaned closer. "Have you asked him yet?"

Meg didn't have to ask Nikki what she was talking about. "No, I haven't had a chance."

"Look, Meg, you've got to help me. I know I'm too young to do it by myself. But I will if I have to. I already know the hospital I was born in in Fort Worth."

Meg felt her panic rising. "Nikki, this isn't wise."

The thirteen-year-old pouted. "How can you say that, Meg? You know who your parents are. So does Linc. I'm the only one who doesn't." Tears flooded her eyes. "I don't even know if I have brothers and sisters out there somewhere.''

Meg could feel her pulse pounding in her throat. Oh God! What was she going to do? she thought, as Nikki sat there looking at her for help.

"You don't know what it feels like not knowing where you come from!" Nikki jumped up and ran out of the room.

Meg started after her but stopped. How could she comfort her? What could she say? Nikki didn't want sympathy. She wanted to find her birth parents. As much as Linc wanted to wait to tell Nikki the truth, the girl wasn't going to allow them that luxury. Meg was going to have to find a way to get Linc off by himself tonight and make him listen to reason.

It took Meg all week to get up the courage, but finally one evening about nine she was in Linc's office. She knew if she waited until they went upstairs to bed, they'd get distracted by other things...like making love.

She paced the room anxiously. How was she going to convince him? Meg knew this was a touchy subject, especially since he and Nikki had gotten close again.

Linc came in the room and closed the door. He smiled and went to her, placing a sweet kiss on her mouth. "This place isn't as romantic as the pool, but it'll do." He leaned toward her again and Meg pulled away.

"Linc, we need to talk."

He frowned. "I know. You mentioned it earlier when you practically summoned me here. What's the problem?"

Meg took a long breath and released it. "Since before the wedding, then after we got home from Dallas, Nikki has been asking me to help her find her birth parents."

Linc looked almost too shocked to speak as he sat down on the edge of his desk. "Tell her you can't."

"It's not that easy, Linc," Meg said, stepping closer.

"If I don't help her, she's threatening to find out on her own."

"No one's going to tell a kid anything. And, anyway, from what my lawyer told me, it was a closed adoption. So don't worry about it." He shrugged. "Nikki will forget about it in a few weeks."

Meg was getting angry. "She's not going to forget about it, Linc. In fact, I've talked with Dr. Hamilton."

"You've told her?"

"Linc, Dr. Hamilton is Nikki's counsellor. She's trying to help us."

He jumped up from the desk. "I just bet. The more people involved... Nikki is sure to find out."

"No, Dr. Hamilton can't say anything, but she told me that Nikki's been thinking about doing this since your parents' death." Meg walked to him. "Linc, I don't think Nikki will forget about it." She looked up at him and their eyes locked. This was the man she loved. Why was it so difficult to explain to him how much she needed to tell her sister the truth? "I think we should tell her."

"No!" He began pacing the room. "She's too young."

"She's grown up a lot in the last year," Meg countered. "And think about what's going to happen if Nikki finds out from someone else."

"The only way is if *you* tell her." His dark gaze bored into her. "Meg, you promised me you wouldn't tell her until I thought she was ready."

"But that was before Nikki started asking questions. How do you think she's going to feel about me when she does find out? I've known we're sisters for the past few months but deliberately didn't tell her. She'll hate me, Linc. And what about our brothers? Clint and Rick have no idea what's going on, either. They're going to be hurt that I didn't tell them. Don't their feelings count?"

Linc hissed out a curse and turned away.

"I stand to lose a lot," Meg continued. "We all do."

The thought crossed her mind that she was already losing her husband. She couldn't bear the thought of losing Nikki, too.

He swung around to face her, his anger evident. "You're not going to lose anything as long as you don't tell Nikki. Remember, Meg, we had an agreement. And I'm going to hold you to it."

His words echoed in her ears, but the pain was in her heart. In one sentence, Linc summed up the reason he'd married her. The only reason.

"That's right, I almost forgot." She fought back the tears. "We did have a business agreement." She had to get out of there, before she made a fool of herself. She started across the room when he grabbed her arm.

"Meg, you know I didn't mean it like that. Our marriage may have started out that way, but now it's different—"

"No, Linc," she interrupted. "You were right the first time. It started out business. It should have stayed that way." She couldn't look him in the eye, her emotions were too raw. "I think it would be best if I move back into my old room."

She waited for Linc to argue the point, but instead his gaze turned icy and unresponsive. He released her. "Fine. If that's the way you want it."

She stared at him, searching his face for any hint of softness. Nothing. She sighed. What choice did she have? "Good night, Linc."

He nodded.

Meg walked out and went upstairs and through the door to her old room. Once inside, she leaned against the wall as her tears overflowed and ran down her cheeks.

Linc Stoner had never wanted a real marriage. He only married her so he wouldn't lose Nikki. He'd only taken her to his bed out of need, never out of love. What about her needs?

Meg sniffed. She wasn't going to turn out like her mother. No man was going to use her, she swore.

No matter how much she loved him.

Chapter Ten

Meg didn't feel like a ride this afternoon, but Nikki had convinced her it would be fun. Josey danced anxiously and Meg leaned forward in the saddle and patted the horse on the neck. "Settle down, girl. We'll be going soon. Come on, Nik," she called into the barn. "Josey wants to go."

There wasn't a verbal response, and instead of Nikki she saw Linc coming out the door. Meg sucked in a long breath and started to look away, but it was impossible to ignore him. He was dressed in a denim shirt that accented his broad shoulders and the familiar faded jeans showing off his trim waist and long legs. Her stomach took a tumble, proving how strong an effect he had on her.

There was no denying how much she'd missed him the past two weeks—or how lonely her nights had been—knowing that he'd never again hold her in his arms. Never make love to her.

She gripped the saddle horn tightly as he approached. When he tipped back his Stetson, she could see the tiny lines etched around his dark eyes. So, he'd lost sleep, too. Since they hadn't been sharing a bedroom, she'd made a point not to come down for breakfast until he'd left the house, and this was the first time she'd noticed how fatigued he appeared.

"Nikki's having a little trouble with her tack. She'll be out in a while," he explained, but he didn't move away.

Afraid to speak, Meg could only nod as the sun beat down on her back. Suddenly it was too hot, and she felt a little dizzy. Swaying, she blinked and tried to focus on Linc. His name was a whisper on her lips as she felt herself slipping sideways, and there didn't seem to be any way to stop herself. She gasped as a pair of strong arms came around her, catching her before she hit the ground.

Linc was terrified as he carried Meg into the cool barn. He pushed open the door to the office and placed her limp body down on a cot. His heart drumming in his chest, he ran to the door and yelled for Nikki. Then he went back to Meg's side and pulled off her hat and loosened her belt.

"My God, Meg. Wake up." He rubbed her hand between his palms, alarmed by her pale face. He left her momentarily and dashed to the small refrigerator, grabbing some bottled water. Pulling a handkerchief from his pocket, he wet it with the cool liquid and pressed it against her forehead.

"Dammit! She shouldn't have been out in this heat."

"What's wrong, Linc?" Nikki came into the room. "Oh my gosh. What happened?" She rushed to Meg.

"Hell if I know." Linc was close to panic. He couldn't let anything happen to Meg. "I went out to tell her what was holding you up and she took a nosedive off Josey. I'm gonna take her to the emergency room. Have Dale bring the—"

Before he got the chance to finish the instructions, Meg groaned and moved her head.

Linc continued to stroke her face. "That's it, darlin', wake up for me."

She blinked several times and finally Linc was rewarded

as her brown eyes looked up into his. He smiled at her.
"How you feelin'?"

"Okay." She tried to sit up but only made it halfway.

"Whoa." Linc pushed her back down.

"What happened?"

"You passed out." Linc continued to grasp her hand. If
only he could hold her. "I think I should take you to the
doctor."

"No, I'm fine. It was only the heat."

"Maybe you ought to eat something," Nikki added. "I
know you didn't have much lunch."

"It was too hot to eat," she argued.

Linc looked down at her shapely body. The first week
of their marriage, he'd gotten to know every curve and
valley intimately. It didn't take him long to realize she'd
lost weight recently. A lot of weight.

"Well, I'm getting you to bed."

Before Meg had a chance to protest, he swung her up
into his arms and started out of the tack room. She had no
choice but to put her arms around his neck and hang on.

"Really, Linc. I can walk."

"You might as well save your energy, darlin'. I'm not
changing my mind," he said as he strode across the yard
toward the house. He sent Nikki on to tell Dora they were
coming.

The girl ran to the house, while Linc carried her effortlessly, and silently. Meg knew there was no talking to him
when he was like this so she decided to enjoy being in his
arms. She laid her head on Linc's shoulder and drew a
long breath of his familiar scent. She was on borrowed
time; as soon as he deposited her in her bedroom, he would
be on his way. Oh, God! She had missed him so much.

By the time they got to the house, Dora was upstairs
pulling back the comforter in the master bedroom. Linc
didn't hesitate as he placed her down on the bed. "But I
should be in the other—"

"Don't worry about it. Get some rest, or I'll change my mind and take you into town to the doctor." He turned and walked to the door. "I'll check on you later."

"I'll bring you some soup, if you like," Dora offered.

"Thanks, Dora. Maybe later. I'd like to rest now."

"Make sure that you do," Linc told her.

Meg nodded and watched as everyone filed out of the room. She dropped her head on the pillow and sighed. What was she going to do now? Nikki had already been asking questions about why she was back in her old room. Now she was here in her husband's bed, and he didn't want any part of her.

She closed her eyes and let sleep take her. She rolled to her side, snuggled against the pillow and decided to worry about it later. Let Linc handle Nikki and her questions.

Linc walked to the barn and away from Nikki, but she had other ideas.

"What's going on?" she demanded.

"Nothing's going on. Meg had a touch of heatstroke and she needs to rest."

"That's not what I'm talking about." She put her hand on her hips. "I'm talking about why she's sleeping in another bedroom."

"Look, Nikki—"

"Don't tell me I'm too young to understand. I'm old enough to see neither one of you is happy."

Linc raised his hand. "We're having a few problems," he admitted.

When her eyes widened, she looked so much like Meg that he had to glance away. "It's me, isn't it," she said sadly.

He saw the tears in his sister's eyes. "No, Nikki. It's just between Meg and me. It's *our* problem."

"But you can't work it out if you don't talk. Remember what Mom used to say. 'If you close a door on someone you love, it's like closing your heart.'" The thirteen-year-old looked desperate. "Please don't do that with Meg. You love her, and she loves you."

Linc closed his eyes. He wished it were that simple.

"Tell Meg you're sorry, and I promise to stay out of your way."

Linc grabbed his sister and hugged her. "Don't you dare. I like having you around. So does Meg. But you can do me one favor."

"What?"

"Stop asking Meg to help you look for your birth mother."

"But—"

Linc placed a finger over her lips. "Nikki, just listen to me. I think you're too young to pursue this. And I think if Mom and Dad were here, they'd agree with me." Tears began to well up in her eyes and it nearly broke his heart. But it would be worse if she walked out of his life. He'd already lost Meg, he couldn't lose Nikki. He removed his finger.

"Will you think about helping me when I'm older?" she asked.

"We'll talk about it—when you're older."

She studied him for a while then finally nodded. "Okay, I'll wait. Now you go upstairs and make up with Meg."

He sighed. "I don't know if that's possible, Nik."

"Please, if you love Meg, you've got to try."

Oh, he loved her, all right, but a lot of good it was doing him. She could barely stand to be in the same room with him.

"Go on." Nikki pushed him toward the stairs. "Go and stay with her. She'd like that."

"I will as soon as I check on Starfire."

She looked at him doubtfully.

"I said I would. Right after I check Starfire," he said, and turned, heading down the aisle toward the back stall.

He lied about needing to see the horse. More likely he needed some time. At least until Meg was asleep. She probably didn't want him in the same room with her, he thought as he worked the latch, opening the stall gate.

The chocolate-colored yearling was still a little skittish around him. Starfire had only been at the ranch a few weeks and wasn't used to his new surroundings yet.

"How ya doin', boy." He rubbed the colt's nose. "A little jumpy?" Linc glanced around the unusually quiet barn. "I know how you feel, fella. It took me a while to get used to things when I first came here, too." He rubbed Starfire's neck. "But it's a great place. Or at least it was before I took over and started messing things up." Before he started taking things for granted. All the years of happiness he had with Joe, Pauline and Nikki. Then one day it was all yanked away from him.

Was that going to happen with Meg? God, he hoped not.

Linc came out of the stall and headed toward the house, all the time wondering how he was going to straighten out this mess. Would he be able to get Meg to forgive him? Could they patch things up and start again, or would she keep closing him out? His pulse soared as he walked into the room and found Meg sound asleep in bed. The air-conditioning had cooled the room and she'd covered herself with the comforter. At least her color had returned, he thought, eyeing the strands of blond hair curled against her cheek. He ached to brush it aside, to touch her soft skin, to kiss... Instead he pulled Pauline's old bow-back rocker from the corner and placed it next to the bed.

He sat down, then leaned forward and watched as the woman he loved slept. Wasn't this what he'd wanted, Meg back in his bed? He'd missed her even more than he thought possible. But he'd messed things up. He studied Meg. God! He never thought he could feel this way about a woman, never wanted a woman the way he wanted her.

But how could he keep from letting their secret destroy his family?

Meg rolled over in bed and stretched lazily, feeling rested for the first time in days. She smiled, then opened her eyes and froze.

Sound asleep, in the chair next to the bed, was Linc. He was still wearing his jeans and shirt from yesterday. She glanced down at herself. For that matter, she had the same clothes on, too. She had slept—she glanced at the clock on the table—nearly fourteen hours. And in Linc's bed. She raised up and suddenly her stomach did a somersault.

Oh, no. Her hand over her mouth, she tumbled out of bed and ran into the adjoining bathroom. She managed to shut the door and make it to the toilet before she got sick. There wasn't much food in her stomach, but that didn't stop her from retching. Finally she collapsed on the floor and closed her eyes, allowing her queasy stomach to settle. This had nothing to do with the heat. She counted back to the date of her last period and realized she was over three weeks late. Given her fainting episode yesterday and the fact that she and Linc made love one night without protection…

Her hand covered her stomach protectively. She was going to have a baby. Her eyes flew open and she smiled. Linc's baby.

"Meg? Are you all right?" Linc called as he pounded on the door.

Meg sat up. "I'm fine." She fought back the queasiness and stood. She pulled open the door to find Linc standing on the other side. A rush of joy brought a smile to her lips. "Really, Linc, I'm fine."

He frowned. "A person doesn't faint for no reason. You're not dizzy?"

"No!" She suddenly felt a lot better. "In fact, I was

about to take a shower." She started past him, when he reached for her arm.

"Why not just shower in here?"

She looked up at his sleepy-eyed look and mussed hair. She wanted nothing more than to take him up on his suggestion. But she couldn't. Not until they'd settled some things. "That's not a good idea, Linc."

"It's the best idea we've had in the past two weeks. You're my wife, Meg. You belong in here with me."

"Your wife? There's no marriage here, Linc. Not a real one, anyway. All we have is a business relationship."

"We could have a marriage, Meg," he suggested. "If you just give it a chance."

"*Me* give it a chance?" She pulled away, but used her finger to jab at his chest. "You're the one who wants everything your way, Linc. You want me in your bed, but you won't even consider my advice about Nikki's interest in finding out about her birth parents."

"I consider your advice about everything but that."

"Can't you understand how important that is to her, Linc? How important it is to me?"

"Telling her that you're her sister wasn't part of the agreement. We both decided to wait. And now she's willing to wait, too," Linc said.

"What do you mean?"

Linc released a long sigh. "Nikki and I talked last night. She thinks she's the cause of our problems. I told her that wasn't true, that you and I have some problems, but they don't concern her."

Meg crossed her arms over her chest. "And what did she have to say about that?"

"She promised to wait until she's older to search for her parents."

Meg didn't look convinced. "For how long?"

"At least a year." Linc's gaze bored into hers. "Now there's nothing stopping us from making this work." He reached for her, and when she didn't resist he cradled her against him. She felt so good. "I meant what I said, Meg. I want this marriage to work, and not just for Nikki's sake. For mine. For ours."

Meg wished that were true. "But how can it, Linc?" She lifted her head to look up at him. "It's built on lies. I can hardly look Nikki in the eye."

"Dammit, Meg, we're not lying. We're just holding off on telling her something that she isn't ready to handle."

Meg started to speak but stopped. She didn't want to argue anymore. "We're never going to agree on this." She turned to leave.

"Where are you going?" he demanded.

Meg swung around and glared at him, unable to ignore the panic she saw in his eyes. Suddenly he seemed as vulnerable as she felt. "I told you, I'm going to shower."

"I mean after that."

"I don't know, Linc." She released a tired breath. "Since Nikki is settled in summer school, I may go visit my brothers." And think about what my future is going to be, she thought. Now there may be a baby to consider.

Meg pulled the Jeep Cherokee into the drive at the Delaney farm. The weathered house looked worse than Meg remembered. The screens on the windows needed to be replaced, along with some of the sagging porch steps.

She got out of the car and glanced around, but there were no signs of life. Why should there be? Even though she had called Clint and told him she was coming, it was the middle of the day. Farmers would be busy working. She walked up to the porch and pushed opened the door that led into the small living room. She smiled on seeing the mess her brothers had left, but all in all the place didn't look too bad.

The worn sofa against the wall had a stack of newspapers next to it. The coffee table was littered with soda cans and milk glasses. The old brown plaid recliner had clothes thrown over the back, but there was nothing a little dusting and vacuuming wouldn't fix.

Well, she'd better get busy. Putting down her purse, she gathered up the clothes off the floor and headed to the small kitchen, where she stopped and gasped. So this was where all the mess was? she thought, eyeing the stack of dirty dishes in the sink. It sure looked like she had plenty to keep her busy until Clint and Rick made it back to the house. But not enough to keep her mind occupied so she wouldn't think about how much she missed Linc. Up until she'd driven off two hours ago, she'd hoped that he would ask her not to go. But he had only told her to drive carefully, then strolled off toward the barn.

Meg dropped the stack of clothes in front of the washer and turned on the water. Adding soap, she began sorting the whites and colors as tears filled her eyes. Feeling she deserved a good cry, she did nothing to stop them from falling.

Two hours later, the house had been straightened and two loads of wash were done. Meg had finished the folding and was checking on the roast in the oven when Clint and Rick walked through the door.

"Boy, with that fancy car out front, we must have a rich relative visitin' us," Clint said.

"Yeah," Rick agreed. "One of those rich horse ranchers."

Meg ran to greet her brothers. "You better be careful or I'll just get in that fancy car and drive back to where I came from." She hugged them both.

Clint stepped back and sniffed. "Not before you get that roast on the table."

"So, it's my cooking you miss?"

"It's a lot more than that," Clint said. "You used to weed the vegetable garden, too."

Meg playfully smacked them both. "Be careful. I'm

thinking about walking out of here and back to where I'm wanted.'' She didn't know where that was anymore.

"Oh no you don't,'' Clint said. "I want you to stay as long as you can. But being a newlywed and all, I didn't think you'd want to leave that new hubby of yours so soon. Trouble in paradise?''

Meg tried to smile, but her brothers knew her too well. Especially Clint.

"Can't I come and visit with my family for a while without you thinkin' there's something wrong?''

Clint raised an eyebrow. "Is there?''

That was all it took. Tears flooded Meg's eyes, and the next thing she knew, her brother was holding her.

"It's gonna be all right, sis,'' he promised. "I knew you got married too soon. Rick and I will go to the ranch tomorrow and gather up your things.''

"No!'' Meg pulled away. "I can't leave.''

They both looked puzzled, but she knew she couldn't tell them. Not yet, anyway.

"Please, just let me stay here for a few days.''

Clint stepped forward. "You can stay as long as you want.'' He glanced at his brother. "We never wanted you to leave in the first place.''

"Thanks.'' Meg knew that whatever their family lacked in material things, they made up for in love. "I just need a few days to think things through.''

"Is Nikki giving you trouble? She seemed pretty attached to her brother.''

"No, this is between Linc and me.'' Her tears started again. "We never should have—''

Clint squeezed her shoulders. "You don't need to talk about it now. Not if you don't want to.''

"Yeah,'' Rick joined in. "Why don't we wait until after we eat?''

In spite of herself, Meg began to laugh. "Is that all you think about?''

The nineteen-year-old stood up straighter than his already six-foot frame. "I'm a growing boy."

"Well, how about driving into town and picking up some groceries?" She handed him a list and some money. Opening her purse, she pulled out her keys and tossed them to him. "Here, drive my car."

Rick let out a war cry. "Thanks, sis." He kissed her cheek and raced out the door.

"He might not be back for hours," Clint said.

"I don't care. Let him have a little fun." She walked to the table and sat down.

"Looks like you could use a little fun yourself. And that fancy horse ranch and a new car hasn't seemed to do the trick." He strode to the table, pulled out a chair and straddled it. "Did Linc turn out to be a jerk? If so, I'll go—"

Meg shook her head. "No, Clint. I just realized you can't make a marriage work without love. I never should have married Linc."

"Then why did you?"

Meg knew she'd promised Linc she'd never tell, but Clint had a right to know. It was unfair to keep her family in the dark, even if they'd never be able to openly acknowledge Nikki as their sister.

"I married Linc for Nikki."

"Didn't have enough misery raisin' us?"

Meg nodded. "Just like I raised you, I wanted to help raise our sister, too."

Her brother looked puzzled.

"Nikki Stoner is our sister, Clint. The baby girl that mom and daddy told us died. Well, she didn't. She was adopted by the Stoners."

After Clint got over the initial shock, Meg spent the next thirty minutes going over the details of how she first found out about Nikki, about their mother's deathbed revelation, about her arrival at the Stoner Ranch and Linc asking her to stay and tutor his sister. How Linc found the birth certificate with the Delaney name on it. About his ridiculous proposal and her promise to keep the secret.

"Linc held all the cards, Clint. I was afraid that I'd never get to see Nikki again," Meg said. "Besides, she really took the Stoners' death hard and I thought I could help." Meg reached across the table and touched Clint's hand. "I'm sorry that I didn't tell you."

"I can't believe that Linc won't let you tell her that she has a family." He stood up. "I mean the girl is asking—"

"He's frightened, Clint," Meg interrupted. "Linc's been around since Nikki came home from the hospital. He doesn't want to lose her."

"Damn!" her brother cursed. "This is all Daddy's fault. And mom. Why did she let him talk her into giving up our baby sister?"

Meg hugged her brother. "That's all in the past, Clint. Right now we have to be concerned with not losing Nikki again."

They discussed going to court and getting visitation rights, but Meg feared that would only make things worse for Nikki.

"So, are you going back to Linc?" Clint asked.

She nodded. "I really don't have a choice anymore. I'm pretty sure I'm going to have a baby."

Chapter Eleven

Linc was up before six. He figured it was useless to stay in bed when he wasn't getting any sleep. He pulled on a pair of jeans and grabbed a shirt from the closet. That was when he noticed the empty side where Meg's clothes used to hang. A sudden emptiness tore at his gut and worked its way up, creating a dull ache around his heart. She'd been gone five days. Five lonely nights. Was this how life was going to be for him? Would Meg ever come home? Would she ever give him a chance to straighten things out?

Hell, he didn't even know how he planned to do that himself. Nikki was being distant again. He knew she was blaming him for Meg's leaving. And she was right. He might not have told Meg to go, but he sure as hell pushed her in the direction of the door.

Now, here he was, all by himself, and hating it. He sank down on the bed that he had once shared with Meg. Their time together might have been short, but now he couldn't stand to sleep in the old brass four-poster without her. Not with the memory of their lovemaking haunting him. The way she had responded to him. The way she had held nothing back. Not like him. He was the one in denial. He was the one who still wanted to keep the secret that threatened their love.

His old man's beatings had taught him how to hide his feelings. Even when Joe and Pauline had taken him in, it had been a long time before he learned to trust them. He smiled despite his misery. With Nikki it had been easy. She had worked her way into his heart from the beginning just as Meg had. He shook his head. He sure could tell they were sisters. And he desperately needed them both in his life.

Now all he had to do was convince Meg that he loved her and make her want to come home. He didn't blame her for leaving. He hadn't trusted her enough to share Nikki, to allow Meg to tell Nikki the truth about her birth mother.

Well, not anymore. He had learned his lesson. Linc got up and walked into the hall. First he was going after Meg to bring her home. Then together they'd tell Nikki the truth. He stopped at his sister's door, quietly turned the knob and pushed it open. He knew it was too early for her to be up, but he needed to check on her. He walked across the floor, the sunlight marking his way to the double bed. The covers were messed up, but to Linc's surprise and shock, the bed was empty.

Nikki was gone. His heart tripped in his chest, then began to race. Where was she? He flipped on the light and searched around the room until he discovered a note on the dresser. He tore it open.

Linc and Meg,
I'm sorry I've caused so much trouble. Maybe if I'm not around you both won't fight anymore, and you'll get back together.

I love you,
Nik

"Dammit, Nikki!" Linc cursed as panic surged through him. He tore down the stairs to the kitchen and found Dora. "Did you see Nikki this morning?" he asked, hoping that his sister had only been gone a short time.

The housekeeper looked up from the stove. "Not since last night. Why?"

He held up the paper in a shaking hand. "She's run away again." He paced as Dora looked over the note. "I've got to go look for her."

"Should we call the sheriff?"

"No!" He protested. "If Social Services gets wind of this, they'll take her away from me for sure this time."

"So you're gonna try and look for her all by yourself," the housekeeper said. "Come on, Linc. When are you gonna stop trying to carry the burden alone? It's about time you opened up enough to let someone get close to you. Trust that sweet wife of yours to help."

He stared at Dora. She was right. Maybe if he'd trusted Meg, she might have stayed around. And if he'd trusted Nikki to handle the news, maybe she'd still be here. He walked to the phone and picked up the receiver.

First Linc dialed the Delaney farm, but no one answered. Next he called the sheriff and reported Nikki missing. After that, he found Dale with several of the hands. They rode out to check the property.

He returned two hours later with no sign of Nikki. He called Meg again, but still no answer. Where the hell was his wife? He then talked to Beth and explained the situation to her. Beth offered to come, but Linc said to wait a few hours and keep in touch. Linc tried to call Meg again. No answer. He hung up the phone, then headed out to his truck. The hell with calling, he had to go look for his sister.

Early that afternoon Meg returned to the farm from her doctor's visit. He confirmed what she had known all along. She was nearly six weeks pregnant. It should have been a dream come true, she thought as she lay down on the sofa, tears filling her eyes. And it would have been, if only Linc loved her. Meg placed a protective hand on her stomach. It didn't matter. She was going to love this child, no matter how its father felt about it.

"Don't worry, baby. I will always be there for you." She thought about what her mother had gone through with Nikki. No child of hers would ever be given up. She had no idea how Linc was going to take the news, but that didn't matter. This was her baby and she already loved him or her.

A car pulled into the driveway and she stood and looked out the window. Oh, God! She found Linc getting out of his truck. What was he doing here?

She struggled with uncertainty even as her hungry gaze devoured him. Dressed in jeans and a tan Western-cut shirt, Linc marched toward the house with that familiar loose-hip gait that made her pulse race. When he pulled off his hat and his black hair fell across his forehead, a warning voice went off in her head. Don't let this man sweet-talk you into anything.

She watched nervously as he walked directly toward the house. Darn. She wasn't ready to face him yet. Brushing her hair back from her face, she straightened her skirt and hurried to open the door. He walked inside without any hesitation.

"Linc, what are you doing here?"

"Nikki. Is she here?" His eyes locked with hers, and he could see the fear and panic in the depths.

"No, Linc. I haven't seen her since I left the ranch."

"Damn! I was hoping she might try to come here. I've checked all the bus stations."

"Nikki ran away?"

He nodded as he pulled a paper out of his pocket. "I found it this morning. She thinks she's the cause of our trouble."

She began to read. "'Maybe if I'm not around you both won't fight...'" Meg waved the note. "This is crazy."

Linc just stared at her. "I need you, Meg. We've got to find her. I know I messed things up, but if you'll just give me another chance..."

Those were the words she had longed to hear, but she didn't have time to listen. They had to find Nikki. "Let me get my things and we'll drive back to the ranch. And when I get my hands on that child, she's going to get a piece of my mind." She looked up at him. "Oh, Linc." Meg gripped his arm as if it were a lifeline. "We've got to find her." She went into the kitchen and scribbled a note for Clint and Rick. "I'll leave my car and ride with you."

"Good, then you can call the ranch on the cellular phone while I drive." He watched her as she prepared to leave. She could see a flicker of pain in his eyes. She wanted to reach out and comfort him. But this wasn't about them. Their problems would have to wait for another time.

"When we find her, we've got to convince her how much we love her and need her in our life," Meg said.

"We've also got to tell her that you're her sister," Linc added. "You were right, Meg. I just hope she doesn't hate me for not telling her about you."

Meg bit her lip to hold back her emotions. "I doubt she'll stay angry with you for long. She loves you too much."

"I pray you're right, Meg."

They walked outside. Linc helped her into the truck and climbed in on the driver's side. "When we find Nikki, I want to bring her back here so she'll be able to get to know her brothers."

As they pulled away, Meg glanced back at the small house, which was in bad need of paint, though the farm was well kept. "She might be disappointed. These are pretty humble roots."

Linc touched her hand. "I know she'll be proud of them. They produced Clint and Rick...and you."

An hour and a half later, having broken the speed limits in both Oklahoma and Texas, they made it back to the ranch. Hurrying into the house, their hopes were dashed when Dora announced, "There hasn't been a word. The sheriff called to check in, but no one's seen any sign of Nikki."

Meg turned to Linc. "How far could she have gone? She didn't have much money, did she?"

Linc shrugged. He wasn't sure. For all he knew, Nikki could have taken some from his desk and he wouldn't know it. He marched into his office with Meg close on his heels. Once behind the desk, he pulled open the drawer where he kept a few hundred dollars for ready cash. "I used to give her a pretty generous allowance until she ran away the first time. But I gave her twenty the last time she went to Julie's." Once behind the desk, he pulled open the drawer and pulled out a stack of twenties. The money hadn't been touched. "It's all here."

"Have you talked with her friend, Julie?"

He nodded. "Before I came after you. Damn!" He slammed his hand on the desktop. "I should have seen this coming. She's been acting strange, spending a lot of time in her room."

"And I shouldn't have left," Meg admitted as she placed her hand on his arm. "Maybe if I'd been around..."

Linc's gaze met her eyes, and he saw the fear in their brown depths. He hated himself because he was the cause. "Look, Meg, I've got to go out and find her."

"I want to go with you," she pleaded.

He nodded, picked up the phone and called down to the barn to have two horses saddled. "They'll be ready in ten minutes." He stared down at her skirt. "Do you have some jeans to change into?'' he asked, reminded yet again of the mess he'd made out of his marriage.

Meg glanced away nervously. ''I still have some jeans upstairs. I'll go change.'' She started out of the room and stopped. ''Is there anywhere close by that Nikki used to go to be alone?'' she asked. ''I remember that Rick and Clint used to hide out at a group of trees by the creek whenever I got angry with them.''

''Just that old cabin up along the ridge. But we checked it first thing this morning.''

Her brown eyes widened. ''Maybe Nikki planned on that.''

Linc frowned. ''What do you mean?''

''It just seems strange to me that no one has seen her. Not along the roads, the bus station, in town. It seems as if she were planning on staying close by.''

Within a few minutes Meg had changed into a pair of jeans and boots, they were on Josey and Ace, heading out of the corral. They met up with a couple of the hands, Harry and Mike.

''We found someone at the cabin,'' Mike said. ''We're pretty sure it's Nikki, but Dale said we should come back and get you.''

''Damn! You were right, Meg.'' Relief rushed through him. ''Where is Dale?''

''He's keepin' an eye on her from the ridge.'' Mike grinned. ''He says to hurry or he'll go down himself, and Miss Fancy Pants won't like what he's got planned.'' Mike held up his hand. ''Those were Dale's exact words.''

Linc couldn't hold back his smile. ''Thanks, guys. I appreciate all your help.''

''Happy to do it, boss.'' They tipped their hats at Meg. ''Sure is nice to see you back, Mrs. Stoner.''

''Nice to be back.'' Meg smiled. ''Mike, Harry, why don't you go to the house. Dora's cookin' a big meal for all the men helping in the search.''

The ranch hands' eyes lit up. "Thanks, ma'am." They rode off.

Meg's horse danced sideways, and she tugged on the reins. "She's safe, Linc."

"At least until I get my hands on her. Come on," he said as they rode up toward the north section of the property, to the cabin. He was angry with Nikki for running away, but he was going to do everything in his power to straighten out this mess. The first thing he was going to do was tell his sister about Meg.

They came over the rise and found Dale waiting for them behind some heavy brush. Meg and Linc got off their horses and tied the reins to the tree next to the foreman's big sorrel.

Dale nodded to Meg, then turned to Linc. "She's inside." He handed Linc the binoculars. "She hasn't moved around much, but I'm sure it's Nikki."

Linc glanced through the lenses but didn't see any activity. "Thanks, Dale. Why don't you go back to the ranch. I'll call you if we need any help."

"Sure." The foreman nodded, climbed on his horse and rode off.

"Do you really think Nikki's been in the cabin the whole time?" Meg asked.

"She wasn't here early this morning when I checked it." He took Meg's hand and pulled her behind him along the edge of the trees. They made it down the small hill. "But there's plenty of brush around here to hide in." When they got close enough to the cabin, they circled around to the back door.

Meg tugged on his arm, getting his attention. "When you confront her, Linc, don't start yelling at her," she whispered. "She's been pretty upset...about us."

"I've been pretty upset, too, darlin'," he whispered against her ear. Then he pulled back and looked into her eyes. "God, Meg! I've missed you." The words came out more like a groan. "I want to straighten things out between us. And the first thing is to tell Nikki the truth."

"Oh, Linc."

Linc wanted nothing more than to pull Meg into his arms, but he had other priorities. He motioned to her that he was going inside, then with a silent prayer he jerked open the door.

He didn't know who was more startled, he or his thirteen-year-old sister, who was huddled on top of her sleeping bag on an old mattress. She looked like a frightened animal.

"Nikki." He went to her as she got up and threw herself into his arms.

"Oh, Linc," she gasped. "I'm sorry. I know I shouldn't have run away, but it's been so awful at the house since Meg went away."

"But Nikki, running away isn't the way to deal with problems," Meg said as she made her way into the small cabin.

"But isn't that what you did?" Nikki accused.

Meg started to argue, then realized Nikki was right. "I guess you've got me there, Nikki," she admitted.

Linc turned to Meg. "I was planning to go after you," Linc volunteered. "In fact, I was on my way to Boswell this morning, when I discovered Nikki was gone."

Meg stared at Linc, wanting to believe him. She finally glanced at her sister. "Nikki, Linc and I have to work things out on our own."

"But I don't want you to go away." Tears started down the girl's face. "I'll never see you again."

Meg cradled Nikki in her arms. "Of course you will." Oh, God, she hoped so. She'd come to love her sister so much.

"Nikki, Meg will always be a part of your life," Linc began, then stopped and studied Meg before he said, "That's because she's...your sister."

The thirteen-year-old blinked. "Sure, because she's married to you."

Linc shook his head. "No, Nik. Meg is your biological sister. Ralph and Nina Delaney were your parents. Meg's your sister and Clint and Rick are your brothers."

Nikki's hand went to her mouth. "But how is that possible? How?"

Meg wiped away her own tears. "Just before my...our mother passed away, she told me about you." God, Meg thought, this was a lot for a teenager to understand. Nikki was so young. "You see, we were poor, and when you came along our father convinced our mother to give you up for adoption." Meg took the girl's hand. "Our mother never wanted to, but our dad made her. He felt it would be best for you and all of us. All those years, our mom wondered how you were. She loved you, Nikki. She asked me to tell you that when I got to meet you. When I came by the ranch to meet the Stoners and learned about the accident and that you were having trouble with their deaths, I decided to hang around and see if I could help."

"Linc—" Nikki glanced at her brother "—you knew, all this time?"

Meg stepped in. "No, Linc hasn't known for very long. At first we couldn't decide when to tell you. But you started asking so many questions..."

Nikki walked across the small cabin to the woodburning stove. Meg followed her and placed her hand on her shoulder. Feeling Nikki stiffen, she removed it. "When you're ready, I'll try and explain...more about our mother and father."

Meg retreated when Linc came over and embraced his sister. Nikki began to cry. It was hard, but Meg held her own needs in check, allowing the two some time to share. She walked out to the porch and looked over the beautiful tree-lined scenery. She drew a deep breath. Oh, how she had come to love it here on the ranch—and the two people inside the cabin. She touched her stomach. Three. There was the baby to think about now.

After a while Linc came out and stood beside her.

"How is Nikki handling it?" she asked.

"Glad that we found her. And sorry she ran away. But mostly confused. It's gonna take some time."

"I was wrong to want to tell her," Meg admitted.

"No!" Linc corrected. "I was wrong. Nikki may be young, but if we'd continued with the lie, she would never have forgiven us." He sighed as he leaned against the rough post railing. "What do we do now?"

"Give her time. Right now she's on the cell phone, calling the house to let them know she's okay."

He turned and looked at Meg, and her stomach did a somersault. If there were a way...

"Nikki's gonna need some time to get used to this, but I know she wants us to be a family," he said.

"We tried that, Linc. It didn't work."

"It didn't work because I didn't let it. I wasn't honest with Nikki, or you."

Hope surged through her. "What do you mean?"

His hands gripped her arms. "Yes, I asked you to marry me because I thought that you could help me keep Nikki. But I was also afraid you'd try and take her away from me."

Meg couldn't believe what he was saying. "That girl is crazy about you." She nodded toward the cabin. "I would never try to break up the two of you. All I ever wanted was to be there if she needed me." *Like I want you to be there for me and our child,* she cried silently.

"I know that now," he confessed. "I was wrong to ask you to lie to her."

He pulled her close and she felt her knees weaken. His lips brushed against her face. "Nikki needs you in her life, and I need you, too. I wasn't honest with you or myself about why I wanted you to be my wife. I love you, Meg.

I know I have a lot to make up for. Just don't push me away."

"Oh, Linc, I love you, too." She reached up and wrapped her arms around his neck. But that wasn't enough. She wanted his touch…his caress. She raised her head and her mouth found his in a tender kiss that soon became heated. He groaned and crushed her to him, convincing her they had a future. "Well, it looks like I'm interrupting again."

They broke apart to find Nikki smiling shakily at them.

Linc still wasn't happy with his sister's little stunt. Though she meant well, trying to get him and Meg back together, she was still in deep trouble.

"I suppose I'm going to be grounded for the next month," she said.

"Sounds about right. And we're going to have a long talk tomorrow, Nik. But right now we're running out of daylight and need to get home."

"Dale's coming out with a horse for me to ride home."

"Good," Linc said, then kissed her. "Now take your sassy mouth and go wait for him up on the hill. Yell down when he shows up."

"Are you kidding? I'm not letting you two horn in on my time with the man I'm going to marry someday," she said teasingly. "I'll ride back to the ranch with Dale, but you two have a few things to discuss alone." She moved past her brother to Meg. "I just want to say goodbye to my sister before I leave." Nikki stood in front of Meg, suddenly shy. "This is all so weird," she admitted. "You're my sister for real. I can hardly believe it."

"I know," Meg agreed, wanting to say so much more. "It took me a while to get used to the idea, but if I had to pick a sister, you'd be it."

Tears filled Nikki's eyes, eyes that were so like their mother's. "Really?" she asked.

"Really," Meg confirmed with another hug. "We'll talk

tomorrow. All day if you want to." She brushed the girl's dark hair back from her face. "Go get something to eat and we'll see you in a while."

They heard a whistle and looked up to see Dale up on the rise. "Isn't he so cute," Nikki giggled.

"Nikki," Linc warned. "You should be looking at boys your own..." he stopped. "Forget it. I don't want any boy around you."

Nikki laughed and hugged her brother. "Don't worry. I'm saving myself for Dale. There won't be any boys hanging around. All you have to worry about is not messing this up with Meg. I don't know how many times I can come to your rescue."

Linc began to wonder if rescuing him had been the real reason for the stunt by Nikki. "I'm getting smarter by the minute," he said. "Now, have you wised up and realized we're a family now, and we love you?"

"Yes, and I love you both," she said, then ran toward Dale and the horses.

They both watched as Nikki climbed on her horse and rode off with the Stoner Ranch foreman.

Linc pulled Meg into his arms. "Now where were we before we were interrupted?" He gave her a lopsided grin that had her weak. "Oh, yeah, here I think." His voice drifted off as his mouth descended on hers.

Meg knew they still had so many things to discuss, but at the moment nothing was as important as the feel of Linc's lips pressed against hers. His mouth was gentle as he nibbled kisses across her cheek, her nose, her eyelids, avoiding her mouth and driving her crazy.

"Did you mean it?" he asked.

Light-headed, she opened her eyes. "Mean what?"

"That you love me."

"Oh, yes."

"Say it again."

"I love you, Linc."

He swept her up into his arms and carried her inside and kicked the door shut. At the bed, he laid her down on the sleeping bag, his mouth caressing hers all the while. "I want you, Meg." He began tugging at her clothes. "I've missed you so badly."

"I missed you too, but shouldn't we be getting back to the ranch?" She worked the buttons on his shirt and pulled it off his shoulders. "Isn't everyone expecting us?"

He kissed her again. "We'll get there eventually." He began to go to work on her jeans and Meg stopped his hand.

"We need to talk, Linc."

"Later."

"No!" She sat up and pulled her blouse together with trembling hands. "There's something I have to tell you. Now."

He gave her a bedroom-eyed gaze and she almost lost her nerve. But they were about to give their marriage a fresh start and she had to tell him. "I'm not going to start college this next year."

He shrugged. "That's okay. I'm surprised, but if you want to wait, I don't have a problem with that."

"Aren't you interested in why?"

Linc was getting impatient. "Well, tell me."

Suddenly it felt as if her emotions were going haywire. Tears pooled in her eyes. What if he wasn't happy about the baby?

"Meg?"

She climbed off the bed and went to the window. The sun was starting to go down in the west. "Maybe this isn't the right time."

He came up behind her and wrapped his arms around her waist. "Meg, what is it? I love you very much. Nothing you have to tell me will change that."

"I'm pregnant," she finally whispered.

He turned her around to face him. She saw the surprise and wonder on his face. "A baby?"

She nodded. "I know it's too soon, but—"

His mouth crushed hers in a kiss that let her know that he was happy about the idea. When they broke off they were both breathless. "God, I love you. A baby! Do you feel all right? I mean, that was the reason you fainted last week, wasn't it?"

"I feel fine." She raised a hand to calm him. "I saw the doctor this morning. He said I'm healthy and there's no reason why I can't have a healthy baby." Her eyes searched his. "I know we've never talked about having a family, Linc. And I can't help wondering how Nikki will feel. How she'll react."

Linc's hand caressed her stomach. He never knew he could feel this way about another person. For the first time in his life he felt he really belonged. "She'll love the baby." His eyes met hers. "This child is going to tie us all together as a family. I love you. I love this child."

"And I love you," Meg said as she reached up to kiss her husband. He stopped her.

"First, promise me one thing."

"Anything."

"Give me a son. I desperately need to even the odds around here."

"Oh, you poor man. I'll see what I can do. If not this time, maybe the next," she promised as he picked her up and carried her back to the bed, making her a few promises of his own.

Epilogue

Meg awkwardly climbed out of the car, relieved that her protruding stomach could still fit behind the wheel. Being pregnant had been the most wonderful experience in the world, but three weeks from her August 10 due date, she was anxious to have the whole ordeal over with.

Swinging the purse strap over her shoulder, she gripped the manila folder in her hand and headed toward the barn to find her husband. She had some great news and couldn't wait to see Linc's reaction when she told him.

The coolness in the barn felt like heaven against her heated skin as Meg made her way toward the inside arena, where she knew Linc would be working. The sound of cheers from the corral and the sight of ranch hands standing along the railing made her wonder what was going on.

Unable to climb up the rungs in her condition, Meg peered through the white slats to find her husband riding Prideful Lady, the mare he'd bought last spring. She saw only Linc's broad back pass by, as he was busy putting the horse through the paces of a figure eight.

Meg smiled. She had always enjoyed watching her husband on horseback, seeing the magnificent animal and man working together. They made a beautiful picture as Linc expertly brought the horse around in a circle. That was when Meg discovered he carried a passenger. Nestled in the space in front of him was their eighteen-month-old daughter, Cassy. The wide, toothy grin was proof that she was thrilled with the ride as her tiny hands raised in the air waving.

Shocked, Meg marched around the arena. Immediately one of the hands opened it, allowing her entrance. The ranch hands began to scatter as she headed through the soft arena dirt toward her husband and daughter.

"Linc Stoner, what are you doing?" she called out.

Guilt written all over his handsome face, he said, "Meg! You're home early." He climbed off the horse, then lifted Cassy into his arms.

"I finished with my doctor's appointment early. And it's a good thing."

"How did it go?" He shifted his daughter in his arms. "You should have let me go with you."

"Maybe I should have. At least I'd know Cassy would be safe." She placed her hands on her expanded waistline.

Linc knew he was in trouble. "Now, Meg, Cassy just wanted to see the horsey. And one thing led to another." Being married to Meg for the past five years, he'd seen her temper flare more than a few times. Usually after a little time alone together in bed, he could usually convince her to forgive him for just about anything. He tossed her his sexiest smile.

"Get those thoughts out of your head, Linc Stoner." She glanced down at the large stomach between them. "Even if I were interested, it's impossible at this stage. So stop trying to distract me. I'm still angry you put Cassy on a horse."

Their curly-headed daughter leaned forward. "See horsey, Mommy." She pointed her chubby little finger.

"Yes, honey, I see a horsey." Meg glared up at Linc. "Seeing a horse is a lot different than riding. Linc, you promised you wouldn't put the children on a horseback until they were at least two years old."

"I know, darlin'. But I was with her. You know that I'd never do anything to hurt our kids."

"But you promised," she said. "That's the only thing I asked of you." She looked at the child. "She's only a baby."

"No baby." Cassy shook her head, then pointed to Meg's stomach. "That baby."

Both Linc and Meg laughed. "That's right, sweetheart," Linc agreed with his daughter. "You're not going to be a baby anymore." He then bent down and kissed Meg. "I'm sorry, Meg." They walked out of the arena and turned over the horse's reins to one of the men. "I'll promise not to take Cassy on any more rides until Christmas."

"Okay," Meg agreed. "But you can't buy her a pony either."

"Wait a minute. How's she supposed to learn to ride?"

"You can strap her on Pauline's pony and walk her around the corral. And that's all." She pointed her finger at him. Linc knew where his daughters had picked up the habit. "And don't you try talking me into letting Pauline get on a horse."

Linc lowered his head, as if already guilty of the deed.

Meg gasped. "You've had her on a horse, haven't you, Linc? She's not even four years old."

"Paulie ride big horsey," Cassy said.

Linc was dead. "Darlin', you know I'd never let anything happen to my daughters. It's just that they're naturals. You saw Cassy up there on Lady. She should have been afraid, but she wasn't. She wanted more."

"More horsey," Cassy repeated.

"Not today, sweetheart." Linc kissed the girl's head and turned back to Meg. "Someday our children are going to be running this ranch. Riding a horse should be second nature.''

''You mean you don't have a problem with your daughters taking over?''

''Of course not.''

''What about Nikki? You seem dead set on sending her away to college next year.''

Linc stopped at the porch steps. There hadn't been one problem with Nikki since the day they'd found her at the cabin. And her 4.0 grade point average could get her into just about any college in the country.

''Looks like you've been talking to her,'' he said. There was no doubt the two had been conspiring against him. He only wanted what was best Nikki. ''Nikki's never been away from home. Maybe she'd like to live on campus.''

Meg cocked an eyebrow. ''And maybe her infatuation for Dale will fade?''

He bent down and kissed her surprised mouth. ''Maybe. I'd like to see her get an education before she gets serious about anyone.'' Pulling open the kitchen door, he set Cassy down. The toddler took off toward her older sister, seated at the table coloring in a book.

''Paulie! Paulie,'' Cassy called out. ''I see horsey.''

The four-year-old, Pauline, looked at her little sister and smiled, reminding Linc of Nikki, though she had her mother's blond hair. ''So what. I'm going to go to school this year.''

Cassy turned to her parents, her lower lip trembling. ''I want to go to school with Paulie.''

''Oh, sweetheart.'' Meg put her things down on the table and managed to lift her daughter on her lap. ''Remember, you're gonna help me with the new baby.''

That immediately stopped any threat of tears and she turned to her sister. ''I get to be a mommy.''

Pauline shrugged. ''I don't care.''

Before things got out of hand, Meg ordered her daughters to go upstairs and play nice together. Pauline took her sister's hand and together they walked out of the room.

Linc pulled his wife into his arms and hugged her as close as her stomach would allow. "Are you sure you don't want to hire a nanny? They're gonna be a handful, and with the new baby..."

"Could you handle another woman in this house?"

Linc gave her a smile that made Meg forget her anger and fall in love with him all over again. "I kinda like being outnumbered."

Meg knew her husband had been thrilled with the birth of both their daughters. And with this pregnancy, they both just wanted a healthy baby. "Well, don't get too cocky. I've got proof here that I'm about to even the odds." She loved the shocked look on his face as she pulled out the ultrasound picture and showed it to him. They both studied it for a while.

"I guess I can finally say that one of my kids will take after me," he said, with such awe in his voice.

Meg smiled and laid her head against his chest. Oh, how she loved this man. "Then I'll be doubly blessed."

Linc looked down at his wife. "No, I've been the one blessed. From the day you showed up at the front door." His mouth found hers in a kiss that promised her love for a lifetime.

*   *   *   *   *

ELIZABETH AUGUST

Continues the twelve-book series—36 HOURS—in November 1997 with Book Five

CINDERELLA STORY

Life was hardly a fairy tale for Nina Lindstrom. Out of work and with an ailing child, the struggling single mom was running low on hope. Then Alex Bennett solved her problems with one convenient proposal: marriage. And though he had made no promises beyond financial security, Nina couldn't help but feel that with a little love, happily-ever-afters really could come true!

For Alex and Nina and *all* the residents of Grand Springs, Colorado, the storm-induced blackout was just the beginning of 36 Hours that changed *everything!* You won't want to miss a single book.

Silhouette®

Take 4 bestselling love stories FREE

Plus get a FREE surprise gift!

As seen on TV!
Free Gift Offer

With a Free Gift proof-of-purchase from any Silhouette® book,
you can receive a beautiful cubic zirconia pendant.

This gorgeous marquise-shaped stone is a genuine cubic
zirconia—accented by an 18" gold tone necklace.

(Approximate retail value $19.95)

Send for yours today...
compliments of *Silhouette®*

To receive your free gift, a cubic zirconia pendant, send us one original proof-of-purchase, photocopies not accepted, from the back of any Silhouette Romance™, Silhouette Desire®, Silhouette Special Edition®, Silhouette Intimate Moments® or Silhouette Yours Truly™ title available at your favorite retail outlet, together with the Free Gift Certificate, plus a check or money order for $1.65 U.S./$2.15 CAN. (do not send cash) to cover postage and handling, payable to Silhouette Free Gift Offer. We will send you the specified gift. Allow 6 to 8 weeks for delivery. Offer good until December 31, 1997, or while quantities last. Offer valid in the U.S. and Canada only.

Free Gift Certificate

Name: _____

Address: _____

City: _____ State/Province: _____ Zip/Postal Code: _____

Mail this certificate, one proof-of-purchase and a check or money order for postage and handling to: SILHOUETTE FREE GIFT OFFER 1997. In the U.S.: 3010 Walden Avenue, P.O. Box 9077, Buffalo NY 14269-9077. In Canada: P.O. Box 613, Fort Erie, Ontario L2Z 5X3.

FREE GIFT OFFER
084-KFD

ONE PROOF-OF-PURCHASE

To collect your fabulous FREE GIFT, a cubic zirconia pendant, you must include this original proof-of-purchase for each gift with the properly completed Free Gift Certificate.

084-KFDR

SILHOUETTE WOMEN KNOW ROMANCE WHEN THEY SEE IT.

And they'll see it on **ROMANCE CLASSICS**, the new 24-hour TV channel devoted to romantic movies and original programs like the special **Romantically Speaking—Harlequin™ Goes Prime Time.**

Romantically Speaking—Harlequin™ Goes Prime Time introduces you to many of your favorite romance authors in a program developed exclusively for Harlequin® and Silhouette® readers.

Watch for **Romantically Speaking—Harlequin™ Goes Prime Time** beginning in the summer of 1997.

If you're not receiving ROMANCE CLASSICS, call your local cable operator or satellite provider and ask for it today!

ROMANCE CLASSICS

Escape to the network of your dreams.

See Ingrid Bergman and Gregory Peck in *Spellbound* on Romance Classics.

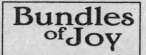

Bundles of Joy

Babies have a way of bringing out the love in
everyone's hearts! And Silhouette Romance
is delighted to present you with three
wonderful new love stories.

October:
DADDY WOKE UP MARRIED by Julianna Morris (SR#1252)
Emily married handsome Nick Carleton temporarily to give her unborn child
a name. Then a tumble off the roof left this amnesiac daddy-to-be thinking
lovely Emily was his *real* wife, and was she enjoying it! But what would
happen when Nick regained his memory?

December:
THE BABY CAME C.O.D. by Marie Ferrarella (SR#1264)
(Two Halves of a Whole)
Tycoon Evan Quartermain found a *baby* in his office—with a note saying the
adorable little girl was his! Luckily next-door neighbor and pretty single mom
Claire was glad to help out, and soon Evan was forgoing corporate takeovers
in favor of baby rattles and long, sultry nights with the beautiful Claire!

February:
Silhouette Romance is pleased to present ON BABY PATROL by
Sharon DeVita, (SR#1276), which is also the first of her new
Lullabies and Love series. A legendary cradle brings the three rugged
Sullivan brothers unexpected love, fatherhood and family.

Don't miss these adorable Bundles of Joy, only from
Silhouette ROMANCE™

Daniel MacGregor is at it again...

New York Times bestselling author

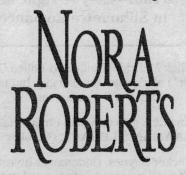

NORA ROBERTS

introduces us to a new generation of MacGregors
as the lovable patriarch of the illustrious MacGregor
clan plays matchmaker again, this time to his three
gorgeous granddaughters in

THE MacGREGOR BRIDES

From Silhouette Books

Don't miss this brand-new continuation of Nora Roberts's
enormously popular *MacGregor* miniseries.

Available November 1997 at your favorite retail outlet.

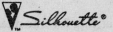

Silhouette®